HAPPILY EVER AFTERLIFE

Ghostcoming!

HAPPILY EVER AFTERLIFE

#1: Ghostcoming!
#2: Crushed

HAPPILY EVER AFTERLIFE

Ghostcoming!

by Orli Zuravicky

SCHOLASTIC INC.

For my mom, who has been
my cheerleader, my makeshift
focus group, and my test reader

Thank you to my parents for supporting me and believing in me—
but mostly for simply being there, always.
Thank you to Kirsten Hall for making this magic possible, to Abby McAden and
Jenne Abramowitz for believing in the paranormal, and to Amanda Maciel for spot-on
editorial instincts and making *my* happily ever afterlife a reality.

ISBN 978-0-545-93256-1

10 9 8 7 6   17 18 19 20

Printed in the U.S.A.   40
First printing 2016

Book design by Jennifer Rinaldi

HAPPILY EVER
AFTERLIFE

Ghostcoming!

LIMBO CENTRAL MIDDLE SCHOOL

Attention: Lucy Chadwick

Your counselor is: Ms. Keaner

Your dormitory is: Jane Austen Cottage, Southampton Hall, Room 312

Welcome to your afterlife education at Limbo Central Middle School!

We hope your crossover journey was a pleasant one, and that you're as excited to be here as we are to have you! The first thing you will notice upon your arrival is that you are mostly see-through. Don't fret. After all, you're a ghost! You aren't a living being anymore, but you still have a body made of energy, and the ability to control energy and manipulate it. We're here to show you how! Just follow all of the rules of Limbo, and we can assure you that in no time, you'll be living your very own happily ever afterlife!

Good luck!

The Limbo Central Administration

THE LIMBO CENTRAL RULES

RULE #1:

You will be able to remember what your life was like and the important people who were in it. Enjoy those good memories as often as you can. However, try as you might, you won't ever be able to remember how or why you became a ghost. So, it's best not to try! Start your afterlife with a fresh, clean slate!

Chapter One
Mr. Perfect Ghost Boy

It's taken me a while to believe it, but the truth of the matter is that I'm dead and there's absolutely nothing I can do about it.

That's right, I'm dead.

Done-zo.

Goner.

A ghost of my former living, breathing self. LITERALLY.

It's not like a woe-is-me thing, I promise. I'm not going to get all sappy and start crying about how much I miss my life, mainly because:

1. I can't *actually* produce tears anymore. (I've tried, believe me.)
2. According to the first Rule of Limbo, I won't ever be able to remember what happened to me, so why bother getting all worked up.

And . . .

3. Because there's no use in crying over spilled blood.

Ha-ha, get it? Blood . . . you know, 'cause I'm dead?

Sorry, just trying out a little ghostly humor.

"Have a seat, Lucy. I'll be right with you," the Limbo Central guidance counselor, Ms. Keaner, says, poking her head out of her office in the administration building of my new middle school.

"Okay, thanks," I say, and head over to the waiting area.

Anyway, I don't mean to be grim (oops, I did it again), just the opposite, actually. I mean, what's funnier than finding out you're a ghost AND that you're stuck repeating your first day of middle school at the same time? Looks like NOTHING will get me out of middle school—not even being dead.

I plop down in one of the comfy armchairs, but instead of plopping, I fall completely THROUGH the chair and crash-land with a big *THUD*. That's right, through the chair.

This day is the worst.

"Chin up, doll. You'll get the hang of it sooner or later," the secretary at the front desk squeaks, looking up from the chart she's reading. She has curly blond hair, red lips, and cat's-eye reading glasses with a silver chain that lets the glasses rest around her neck when she's not wearing them. She looks like she just stepped out of an old movie. "You can't sit because, well, look at you! Right now, you're basically a hologram."

"Yeah," I say, looking down and through myself. She's completely right. I *am* basically a hologram. A mist in the shape of my old self. What it would look like if the *idea* of me got up and started walking around. "It's not as cool as I always thought it would be," I say. "Being a hologram, I mean."

There's a momentary pause, but she says nothing, so I continue. "So . . . do I just have to stand up for the rest of my life—I mean, death?"

"Afterlife, dear. It's less drab."

"Okay . . . so, do I just have to stand up for the rest of my afterlife?"

"You can pretend to sit until you get the hang of it," she remarks, but it's clear from her tone that it's all pretty much just for show. "People find pretending less awkward, you know, in public."

"Excellent. Less awkward is definitely what I'm going for. Thank you," I say, and I situate myself about an inch over the cushion of the chair in a seated position. I look down at the table next to me and see a handful of magazines fanned out. *Celebrity Ghosts, HEALTH & SHAPEshifting, Paranormal Style.* I notice *Medium* magazine's headline—"Limbo's Top Ten Most Wanted Apparitions"—and reach for it. I want to take my mind off of what is happening right now and pretend for a moment that things are normal. Then I remember that I can reach all I want but I can't touch.

I'm distracted by the creaking sound of the main door as two loud girl ghosts walk into the administration office. They are both categorically less invisible than I am, and as they waltz in, the scent of trouble fills the room like a bag of burnt microwave popcorn. They look completely normal and are touching the ground with their feet.

I'm immediately envious. I lose my concentration and before I know it . . . *SPLAT!* I fall straight through the chair again.

"I thought ballerinas were supposed to be *graceful,*" the prettier girl remarks, looking right at me. She has long black hair with bangs cut straight across her forehead, cherry-red lips, and blue eyes. "But she's even sadder than I expected— tights, tutu, and all!" she continues, laughing to her friend.

Did I forget to mention that I look like I just broke out of a Russian music box? Yeah. One minute I'm practicing for my ballet recital—that much I remember—and the next thing I know, here I am stuck permanently in a black leotard, pink tights, pointe shoes, and a white tutu.

"Little miss goodie *toe* shoes," the blue-eyed mean girl concludes.

"I know I can't sit as well as I used to," I call out, "but I can still hear just fine."

I may be new to Limbo Central and the way of afterlife and everything, but I'm not new to the first day of middle school, and I'm not new to the phenomenon of the Mean Girl. Alive or dead. Well, that's not entirely true; I *am* new to *dead* mean girls. But they're basically the same thing as live ones, right?

Give or take a breath.

All I'm saying is, I had my fair share of mean girls in the land o' tutus and blisters. I learned how to defend myself after a while.

"I'm sorry, but did you just say something?" she asks, even though she knows exactly what I said. "I couldn't hear you over all of that tulle."

Just then, Ms. Keaner's office door opens and someone gorgeous walks out. Mean Girl and I both lose focus.

And possibly our minds.

A boy. A ghost. A boy ghost. But mostly a boy (I think, although I'm not sure I'm fully qualified to say which outweighs which yet) appears in the office. A tall, not-at-all-see-through, sandy-haired boy with green eyes and a smile that says, "Hi, my name is Perfect and I tutor orphans and rescue endangered species in my spare time," comes strolling out, and for a moment I think, *How can afterlife possibly get any better?!*

"Come on in, Lucy," Ms. Keaner says.

Swell timing, o ye guidance counselor of mine. I float past Mr. Perfect and hope he doesn't notice my ridiculous outfit. There's, like, a 10 percent chance he won't.

Okay, 1 percent.

(Fine, 0.5 percent.)

"Welcome to Limbo," Ms. Keaner says as she ushers me over to the chair beside her desk. I assume I'm supposed to hover over it, pretending to be seated again, so I do. "Our world is also known as the Ghost or Spirit World, but we prefer Limbo. It's more whimsical, don't you think?" she adds with a smile.

"Um, sure," I remark, trying to stop thinking about the boy ghost. There are way more important matters at hand. "So, Ms. Keaner, where am I going to be living now?"

"The dormitories. Your dorm is listed right on your welcome letter, but don't worry about that yet. We'll have everything set up for you after school," she replies. "There are a few skills you'll need to conquer before you can fully function like everyone else, but most ghosts pick them up like that!"

She finishes her sentence with a snap of her fingers. A real one that makes noise and everything. "Limbo Central Middle School operates just like any other school. We have rules and we expect you to adhere to them. They are all in the *Limbo*

Central Handbook. If you have any problems, you are to come and see me immediately. It will take you a little time to catch up to the rest of your classmates, but we have reviewed your time in the World of the Living and have no doubt that you will catch on quickly."

I know there are words coming out of her mouth and I'm fully capable of understanding them, but I can't stop thinking about Mean Girl and Mr. Perfect Ghost Boy long enough to process what she's saying. Seeing them in the office made me realize that today is my one and only chance to make a good impression and change the course of my life—I mean, afterlife.

The thing is, I wasn't *exactly* popular at my old school. I had my best friend, Felix, and a few girlfriends in some of my classes, but I was a ballet dancer (in case you didn't pick that up), and ballet dancers don't have time to do anything that normal people do. Which means we don't have normal friends—we have dancer friends. Cecily Vanderberg was my closest girlfriend at the studio, but even she was secretly happy when I sprained my ankle and she got to take over my solo in last year's spring recital.

"Lucy, you look troubled," Ms. Keaner says after more moments of silence. "What's on your mind?"

As if I can narrow it down to just one thing. I quickly redirect my thoughts toward things that Ms. Keaner can actually help answer—and wow, are there a lot.

"Well, for starters, am I going to be wearing this ballet costume for the rest of my afterlife?" I ask. "And why am I more see-through than you and everyone else? How do I get more solid so I can sit and walk and touch things like a normal ghost? Will I ever age, or will I be like this forever?"

Ms. Keaner, to her credit, looks unaffected by the clown car of questions that tumbles out of my mouth. No doubt she's heard all of them hundreds of times before.

"Your questions will be answered soon enough, I promise you," she says calmly. "In no time, you'll feel completely natural being a ghost. The classes here at Limbo will teach you everything you need to know, and we offer new students special guidance for their first week here, so don't worry about a thing! Right now, just try to sit back and enjoy your first day at Limbo Central!"

She gives me another big smile.

"I can't sit back," I point out. "I'll fall through the chair."

"Right, well, it's just an expression, dear."

"Ms. Keaner, I am completely and totally unprepared to leave this room!" I cry out with utter honesty.

"Most young ghosts feel exactly the same way, but nonetheless, you must be strong and brave," she replies, still calm. "I promise you, this will be no different than the first day you started middle school in the World of the Living."

Well, isn't *that* a relief?!

Worst. Pep talk. Ever.

"But my first day at Parker Reilly Junior High was the worst day of my life!" I screech. "Felix and I didn't have any classes together and at lunchtime I got stuck at a table between Pete the paste-eater and Mary-Sue Glenning, the girl with so many allergies that they had to monitor the lunches of the people who sat *next* to her! Apparently, she had no allergy to paste, but peanut butter was the kiss of death. If only I'd brought peanut butter and jelly that day, but no luck there." I pause to take a breath. "I mean, if today is anything like that, well . . . well . . . I would normally say 'kill me now!' but I guess that doesn't really apply here, does it?"

"Hmm," Ms. Keaner says, looking deep in thought. "I must stop equating the two school experiences from now on, I can see that. But it's going to be fine, I promise you. As I said, in addition to your regular school classes, you will be assigned a tutor for the next week—an older student who can help you grasp some of the skills you'll need to get around on your own. Your assigned tutor is waiting outside my office for you right now, so you won't be alone."

Then I have another thought. A horrible, frightfully disturbing, very bad thought. What if my tutor is blue-eyed crazy pants out there?! Please, please, pretty please, Ghost Powers That Be . . .

We walk back out into the main office and to my relief, the mean girl and her sidekick are nowhere to be seen. I'm so focused on making sure she isn't around, that I completely overlook the ghost who is.

"Lucy Chadwick, this is Colin Reed," Ms. Keaner says, introducing Mr. Perfect Ghost Boy from earlier. "Here is your schedule, and these are your books," she continues, handing them to Colin. "He'll be carrying your things for you until you are strong enough to carry them yourself."

"Hey, Lucy," Colin says, smiling.

I extend my hand to shake hello, and he slowly extends his, too, cautiously, like he's confused about my plan.

This should faze me, but it doesn't.

I reach over, and because I am so intent on producing a nice, strong handshake to show how awesomely confident I am, the force of my swing-and-miss throws me shoulder first into Colin's chest as if I am tackling him at the twenty-yard line.

Except that I don't *actually* tackle him because I CAN'T DO THAT EITHER! So I pass right through his chest and *BOOM*! I wind up floating flat on my face an inch away from the floor. I literally just threw myself on the ground for no apparent reason.

Mortified.

"I'm sorry," I mutter, wishing I had remembered that I

can't perform most of the things I learned to do by the age of six. "That was so stupid of me. Oh, god, I went right through your body, didn't I? Talk about an invasion of privacy . . . I'm sorry, I'm so sorry."

If my face weren't completely see-through, it would be bright red right about now.

"Don't worry about it," he replies, laughing. "It happens to all of us when we first get here. It took me almost two months to learn how to change my clothes—don't be so hard on yourself. Come on, let's go find your first class."

Okay . . . so, things *could* be worse. Having Colin carry my things, show me around school, and teach me the ropes one-on-one doesn't sound half-bad, right? Then again, it's only Day 1 of my new life (I mean, *afterlife*), so I could still be wrong.

Dead wrong.

THE LIMBO CENTRAL RULES

RULE #2:

New ghosts must alter their own appearance with no assistance. You may only use the energy that you harness through your own powers and strength to effect these types of changes. This is an important skill for any ghost to learn, and we insist that you take it seriously. No student shall alter another student's physical appearance or he/she shall deal with the grave consequences of said action.[1]

[1] Warning: Using your powers on another ghost for any reason takes double the strength and energy, and often results in extreme exhaustion and the dilution of your own powers for a period of time.

Chapter Two
Insert Invisible Foot Here

Following first period (Famous Apparitions), and second period (Debunking Strategies 101), I finally have a normal class. Well, maybe not *exactly* normal, but one I can at least understand and follow logically: P.E., or Psychic Education.

"Ladies, the game is volleyball," Coach Trellis says. "Focus on getting the ball over the net, and scoring on your opponents. Really control your energy intake and output here. You have ten minutes to warm up, and then we're going to have a nice, clean game. Oh, and we have a new student, Lucy Chadwick. Lucy can't participate yet, but she'll be over here observing."

Coach Trellis points to the side of the net where one of the teams is warming up, throwing the ball back and forth, and sends me over there. Of course, it's just my luck that Ms. Blue-Eyed Mean Girl and her partner in crime are in my class and on my assigned side of the net.

Oh goody.

"Look at what we have here," Evil Blue Eyes says, slyly moving to one side of me while Blondie positions herself on the other. "Hey, Ballet Barbie, catch!" she continues.

Then—*WHISHH*!! She throws the ball right through my head!

THROUGH MY HEAD!!!

"What are you doing?" I yell, for lack of something wittier. A ball just soared through my brain, so I'm gonna go ahead and cut myself some slack on that one.

"I said, *catch*," she replies.

Her snark factor is off the charts.

"Oh, that's right," she continues. "You can't. Because you're completely useless."

I look around to find Coach Trellis and see that she's at the door of the auditorium talking to another teacher. Perfect. Not that I want her help, or anything.

"*I'm* useless?" I shoot back, trying to sound way less frustrated than I feel. "You're the one throwing balls through my head!"

"*I'm* sorry, but I don't know what you're talking about."

"Yeah," says the sidekick. "Georgia was warming up, throwing the ball. Just like Coach said."

"How did I manage to get on your blacklist after three seconds of being dead?" I shoot back, though it sounds more whiny than intimidating.

A few other girls have started watching us, but no one comes to my defense. Obviously everyone here thinks Blue Eyes—I mean Georgia—is awful, but they're also too afraid to stand up to her.

It is so wrong that super mean girls even have friends, that people find them remotely enjoyable, that no one ever sees through them.

No pun intended.

Georgia doesn't say anything and I'm so mad that I don't even notice the next ball flying directly at my face until it's a few inches away. As it zooms at me, I brace my hands to catch it—as a matter of habit—but instead of going straight through my hands, the ball suddenly halts in midair! Then it bounces back a little, like it hit an invisible rubber wall. I feel a kind of electric shock pinch my palms as the ball runs up against them, which sends a current swooping through my entire body. I feel almost alive again. The ball just hangs there for a second, like it's unsure of what to do next, and I can't stop staring at it. I don't know if I'm keeping it afloat or if it's just doing it on its own, but the second I blink it falls to the ground.

Through my feet.

"Oh my god, did you see that?" some girl loud-whispers.

"I couldn't do that for a month!" someone else says, though I can't tell if it's out of praise or jealousy.

"Look!" another voice cries out.

The room erupts in more questions and shocked expressions, until all I can hear is the soft, blurry buzz of airy voices all around me.

But no one is more surprised than I am. I look down and notice that my "current state of solidity" (as Ms. Keaner calls it) has shifted. I don't know what percent of me is solid now, but I'm visibly less transparent. I'm also suddenly exhausted.

I have no idea what just happened, but whatever it was stops everyone in their tracks, including Georgia.

"What's going on?" Coach Trellis calls, finally finished with her private conversation and able to rejoin the class.

No one says a word. With all eyes on me, I think briefly about ratting my new friend Georgia out, but decide to stay silent. I'd rather scare her off myself than raise an army of teachers to do it for me, and for some reason my ball-stopping abilities and slightly increased solidity appear to be tipping the scale in my favor.

At least for now.

When I get out of my fourth period History of Paranormal Activity class, Colin is leaning against the wall, waiting for me by the door to my classroom. He keeps brushing his hair away from his eyes with one hand, which is when I notice the silver ring he's wearing on his middle finger.

This makes my heart squeal. Everyone knows that boys who wear silver rings are totally existential (aka super sensitive and thoughtful!). He's also wearing this professional-style camera slung across his chest, which makes him look all creative and artsy.

We make eye contact as I reach the doorway, and I'm excited to use my carefully crafted opening line.

"I like your—"

Then I notice Georgia eyeing me from across the hallway and I lose my train of thought.

"You like my . . . *what*?" Colin says, intrigued.

I get nervous and switch tactics. "Uhm, I like your punctuality. Right on time, mister!" I reply, and pretend to tap my wrist awkwardly as if it's olden times and we're playing a game of charades.

Pathetic.

Colin laughs. The kind of laugh that says, "This girl is a big ol' bag of crazy." Then he heads into the classroom to collect my books.

"Ready for lunch?" he asks.

Oh goody. I'm starving (jeez, I hope ghosts eat!) and in serious need of a break.

"Ready," I say.

"So, how's your first morning at Limbo?" Colin asks me as we make our way down the hall.

"On a scale of one to ten—one being the worst, ten being the best—I'm going to go with a .009, give or take a one thousandth."

"Aha!" he cries out triumphantly. "That's *not* a number from one to ten."

"Math prodigy, table for one!" I joke back.

"Right. I'm lame, sorry," he says. "Why's it been so bad?"

"Well, every time I forget that I can't touch anything and I try to open my book or pick up a pen, people explode with laughter. And, I mean, I literally saw someone explode from laughter—which is super weird by the way and we'll have to get into that more later—and someone moved my chair in Debunking 101 without me noticing and when I finally looked down I was hovering right through the middle of the desk and I didn't even know it! Oh, and this horrific mean girl who I met earlier this morning is in my third period P.E. class, and she and her evil sidekick just kept throwing balls through my head. THROUGH MY HEAD! I mean, really? Of course, she pretended she wasn't doing it on purpose, but she can't fool me. And, actually, that's when something kind of strange happened."

I'm not sure why I confide in Colin, exactly. I guess I've been a lot lonelier here than I expected. And it's only been, like, six hours! I can't imagine going on like this for much longer. I feel like my brain is about to burst, which doesn't exactly seem like a medical emergency here, but I'm pretty sure if it did, the *embarrassment* alone would kill me all over again!

Besides, Colin *is* my tutor for the week, so if anyone can help me sort this out, he can. Guess I might as well tell him everything.

"I couldn't help but notice you look less invisible than you did three hours ago," he says when I've finished my horror story, "but I wasn't sure if you knew. I didn't want to say anything to freak you out."

"Oh, don't worry. I've got freaking out covered all on my own," I reply.

"Okay, then. Well, the good news is that everything you told me is actually really great," he says, trying to be reassuring. "You're a lot stronger than you think. And a lot more powerful than most of the kids I've seen here. The more you learn, the more it'll make sense. You just have to be patient."

"I don't know—judging by how everyone in my class reacted, you'd think I was a total leper. At this point, it can only go up from here, right?" I add a smile, trying to look sweeter than I feel.

"Nice tights, *Swan Lake*!" some burly kid screams out as he passes me in the hallway, which elicits laughter from every angle.

I stop smiling. This outfit is like wearing a bull's-eye on

my back that says, "Fire away!" It's basically impossible to be invisible while you're walking down the hallway wearing a tutu. And I like being invisible sometimes.

"Actually, I take that back," I say, raising an eyebrow at Colin. "That's probably the twentieth time this morning someone's made fun of the tights, which brings my ranking down to a whopping .007."

"Don't take it personally," he says, with the coolness of a movie star. "That's just Jonah. He's like that with everyone."

"A friend of yours?" I ask, surprised.

"I feel like the wrong answer will get me in trouble," he jokes.

"Oh, I'm sorry," I reply, not realizing my tone. "It's not like that. I mean, he *did* just humiliate me in the hallway in front of hundreds of students on the first day of the rest of my after-life," I say with fake casualness, "but I'm sure he's a swell guy and all."

"He's just a clown," Colin insists. "You'll like him once you get to know him. Would it make you feel any better if I told you what I was stuck wearing when I got here?"

"Exponentially, I'm hoping."

"Okay," he says, with a smirk, but then his face gets serious. "But I warn you, if you tell anyone about this I'm going to have to kill you."

I burst out laughing. "As long as you let me choose a better outfit first."

He laughs too. "Deal."

"Okay, now spill it," I continue.

"All right, all right. When I crossed over I was dressed as Boba Fett."

"Bless you?"

"Very funny."

"Okay, so . . . I'm guessing I'm supposed to know what a Boba Fett is?"

"You can't be serious!" he replies, outraged. "You have to have seen *Star Wars*? You know, 'A long time ago in a galaxy far, far away . . . ' "

I say nothing.

"Every human being—alive or dead—has seen *Star Wars* at one point or another and knows who Boba Fett is. Those movies are so classic that my dad has them on *video*—you know, what old people used before DVDs?"

"Not this human," I say, feeling embarrassed. "Not alive and not dead. Not on old-people video, or DVD, or anything."

"That decides it, then. You must be an alien."

Then he does some fancy footwork with his hands (I guess that makes it fancy handwork) and conjures up a hologram in midair—which is see-through, kind of like me—of what looks like a toy action figure wearing armor from head to toe, including this full-coverage mask-helmet thingy that completely covers the face.

"This is Boba Fett—the most revered bounty hunter in the whole galaxy," he says. "I must have been going to see one of the new movies. That's the only time I would get dressed up like that."

"So . . . you're a big nerd, then?" I say with a smile.

"Very funny, *Swan Lake*. It was the worst thing to cross over in. I couldn't even take off the helmet. People didn't know what I looked like for two months."

"But didn't most people know who you were dressed up as? I mean, since every other human has seen *Star Wars* but me, didn't they just pat you on the helmet and tell you how awesome you looked?"

"Not exactly," he says, and I can see him blushing.

"Come on, spill."

"Okay, fine. Yes, some people thought I looked awesome. But only the hardcore *Star Wars* fans. No one else would come near me! It was really embarrassing. I mean, just because I like *Star Wars* doesn't mean I want to talk about it twenty-four hours a day or walk around school dressed like a bounty hunter."

"I'll give you that," I admit. "You should try walking around dressed like a ballerina—it is *so* delightful."

He chuckles. "Anyway, there you go. I still think my story is worse than yours, and remember, it took me two months to get out of it!"

"So they're really serious about no one being able to change our clothes for us, huh?" I ask. "We have to do it all ourselves?"

"Technically, someone *could* alter another person's appearance if they harnessed enough energy, but it's definitely against the rules. I guess they figure if someone did it for you, you'd have no reason to learn. It's kind of like a rite of ghost passage."

We walk into the cafeteria and I get flashbacks from my *first* first day of middle school. I don't know what I'm more worried about—whether or not I'll be able to eat, or who I'll be stuck sitting next to if Colin chooses to ditch me.

Not that I would blame him. (Okay, I'd blame him a little.)

"I usually sit over there . . . See that table all the way in the back corner?" He points to the other side of the room and I scan as quickly as I can to get a sense of his crowd.

Based on his Boba Fett story, I expect to see a bunch of boys with glasses and T-shirts that say things in Klingon and have pictures of SpongeBob or Einstein on them. Don't get me wrong—I don't mean any of this in a bad way. Nerds are awesome. Felix's favorite television show is *Doctor Who*, and even though I refused to partake in any of his sci-fi activities, I love that he loves that stuff.

But at Colin's table I see a bunch of kids who look like they stepped out of a Hollister catalog, a couple of muscle-y guys (including Jonah) wearing various professional athletic jerseys, and out of the corner of my eye, I swear I catch a glimpse of Georgia's sidekick, but I hope I'm wrong.

"Those are your friends?" I ask.

"Well, they aren't my *only* friends," he replies. "But yeah. Let's go get some food."

"So ghosts *do* eat?" I ask, wanting it to sound more sarcastic than it actually does.

"Yeah, we eat. Food gives you energy, and you're going to need it. A lot of it. Otherwise, you'll stay this see-through forever and you won't be able to do anything, pretty much."

We go through the food line and Colin piles his plate high with everything from chicken fingers to mashed potatoes to pie. But he suggests that I just get a fruit-and-yogurt smoothie and puts one on his tray for me.

"So, your boy-plate is fully loaded with every delicious food under the sun and my girl-plate consists of one sad, lonely fruit smoothie?" I say, skeptically. "This is looking an awful lot like the start of an afterschool special."

"Trust me," he says. "I would love nothing more than to watch you devour a plateful of meatloaf and pie in your tutu, but you're not ready. A smoothie is the only thing you'll have the strength to ingest. Even if you can manage to pick it up, you'll have to work really hard to get it into your mouth to convert it. Eventually you'll be able to eat three pieces of pizza, a bucket of fried chicken, and an entire pint of ice cream if your heart desires it," he promises.

"Well, my heart might desire it, but this leotard sure doesn't," I reply.

"Oh, did they not tell you food here doesn't change how you look? I mean, aside from making you look more or less see-through. It's just an energy thing."

Say *what* now?

Afterlife just got *infinitely* better than life.

"I'm sorry, I don't think I heard you right. Did you say ghosts can't gain weight?" I confirm, just to be sure.

"Nope. Just like we can't age, we can't get heavier or thinner either. More food makes our abilities stronger, less food weakens us. That's all."

"Okay," I say. "I can get behind that logic."

As we walk through the cafeteria, Colin points to the different groups of people clustered at their respective tables, and I realize how very similar life and afterlife really are.

"Limbo has its cliques just like every other school," Colin begins. "It's totally predictable, but that's afterlife, I guess. Ghosts can be divided into five main categories, although you could argue that here, at least, there's one main category, and then four subsets."

"Did you want to draw me a Venn diagram?" I say, smirking.

"Maybe later."

We make our way through the cafeteria as he's giving me my first lesson in ghost social politics, and I try my best to divide my attention between listening and gliding as gracefully as possible.

All eyes are on me: the new girl. Or, should I say, all eyes are *through* me. Colin's right . . . I can't even touch the ground, how am I going to lift my lunch, let alone eat it?! What if I spill the smoothie all down my leotard because I can't find my mouth? I think being new is even worse than being dead. Seriously.

And it's not even one o'clock yet.

"Most of us are Intelligent Spirits," he tells me. "Some of us are more intelligent than others, though," he says, pointing to a table all the way in the front of the room.

I look over and see six guys who are wearing matching T-shirts that say GHOSTS = ½ M (MASS OF OBJECT) V (SPEED OF

OBJECT)^2 and playing chess with a holographic board and game pieces.

"Nerd spirits, check!" I repeat.

"Next up, you have your classic Poltergeists." He nods in the direction of the table on our left, filled with delinquents. One kid is aiming spitballs at random ghosts across the cafeteria, while another has created a catapult with her spoon and is currently shooting blocks of Jell-O at the ceiling to see how long they will stick. A second passes before a pile of cherry-flavored goop falls from the sky and finds its way right onto Colin's tray.

"Our resident troublemakers. They are always in and out of the principal's office, constantly getting suspended, you know the type."

"Fascinating," I say. "Who's next?"

"Recurring Haunters."

I look over and see a table full of dark, black-haired, black-nailed kids with sad eyes and giant platform shoes. One kid is drawing on a girl's arm with a marker, while another sits huddled over a copy of *Dracula*.

"The Shadow People sit at those four tables over there," he says, and points to tables full of different athletic groups, which spill over onto the original table he pointed out as his own. Football players, basketball players, soccer players, lacrosse players, even wrestlers.

"Obsessed—and I mean *obsessed*—with sports," he says.

"School spirit, rah, rah!" I say sarcastically.

"And last but not least, the Doppelgangers." He points to the table next to the chess players. "Our resident drama queens."

I look over and I see a table mixed with guys and girls who each seem to be totally in their own world. Some of them are singing, some are sitting on each other's laps, and at least two of them appear to be holding what look like scripts and reciting lines back and forth while a slew of friends listen intently. Just then, one of the girls reciting lines stands up and offers the crowd a bow. They all clap. When she stands back up, I see she is wearing a T-shirt that says ACTING IS MY AFTERLIFE.

"Here we are," he says, sitting down at the table he pointed out earlier as his.

"And which group do you guys belong to?"

"The super-awesome, totally normal, and non-nerdy Intelligent Spirits group."

"Ha-ha."

The moment we sit down, a lady approaches the front of the room with the microphone in hand.

"Who's that?" I whisper.

"That's the principal, Ms. Tilly," he says.

"Please be seated and quiet down everyone," Ms. Tilly says soothingly into the microphone. "I know you have all been waiting patiently for weeks to find out more details about our Limbo Central Middle School Ghostcoming weekend festivities—and here to tell you all about it is our supremely talented party planner extraordinaire and head of the Ghostcoming committee, Georgia Sinclaire."

The school claps as I see my nemesis—Ms. Blue-Eyed Crazy Pants herself—approach the stage.

I lean in to Colin and whisper, "Say hello to the person who spent all of third period hurling balls through my head. She's gotta be a Poltergeist, right?"

He looks at me like I just kicked his dog. *Ouch*. I feel like I've just stepped over some invisible line in the sand, but I'm not sure where it is or how I've crossed it. Maybe being a Poltergeist is more serious than I imagined? Maybe I shouldn't be joking about it . . .

I start to ask him if I've said something wrong, but Georgia's voice is suddenly blaring through the microphone, so I stay quiet.

"Thank you so much, Ms. Tilly. Exactly one week from Friday we will celebrate Ghostcoming with a football game between Limbo Central Middle School and North Limbo Junior High at 6:00 PM, followed by the Ghostcoming dance on Saturday, starting at 7:00 PM. This year's theme will be Famous Couples in Literature!"

Whispers break out across the gym.

"Find your perfect partner and get ready to dance!" she continues. "This year's dance is special because it's not *only* a dance—it's a dance-a-thon! The winning couple will be crowned Ghostcoming king and queen! You must be part of a famous couple from literature in order to participate in the dance-a-thon."

Georgia stops talking and the room gets loud again. Everyone is buzzing about the big Ghostcoming plans. I would be, too, if I weren't automatically annoyed that a) Georgia is in charge of the whole thing, and b) I can't dance unless I'm half of a *couple*. Dancing is my thing! Of course, I can't even do that here without a date—and who's going to ask the new girl in the tutu who can't change her outfit to the Ghostcoming dance?

No one, that's who.

"Boy, she's a piece of work," I say to Colin. "Pretending to be all sweet and school-spirit-y when all she's *really* trying to do is make everyone here without a date feel like a giant loser! And did I mention she spent the better half of the morning throwing balls at my head? I swear, the second I can actually lift a ball, I'm returning the favor!"

I'm so distracted by my rant that I completely miss someone sneaking up behind us at the table. I only notice there's someone there when I see hands covering Colin's eyes from behind him.

"Guess who?!" the voice squeaks.

I turn around and there she is, Georgia Sinclaire in the flesh. Well, not really in the flesh, but you get my point.

"Hey, Georgie," Colin says, sweetly.

Georgie?!

"Have you met Lucy?" he continues, taking her hands off his eyes and allowing them to lay across his chest.

"Nope, not yet!" she replies, cheerily lying through her teeth. "I mean, we had P.E. together this morning but we didn't really get a chance to meet. Welcome to Limbo Central! I'm Georgia, Colin's girlfriend."

"Of course you are," I reply.

This is unbelievable.

I may still be too see-through to eat solids, but apparently I have no trouble whatsoever putting my invisible foot in my mouth.

THE LIMBO CENTRAL RULES

RULE #3:

Ghost housing is predetermined based on a variety of factors. Male and female housing buildings are separate and students are restricted to their respective buildings at all times.

Please note: New students have added energy in their rooms to aid them in the usual comforts that they otherwise would not be able to achieve at first.[1] These energies can be adjusted and deflated on your Tabulator as you learn and perfect your spirit skills.

[1] *Yes, it is against the rules* to use this extra energy to change your physical appearance.

Chapter Three
Once Upon a Frenemy

"Have a seat, Lucy," Ms. Keaner says. "I'll be right with you."

It's 3:05 PM, and even though my first day at Limbo Central is officially over, I'm once again sitting in the administration office waiting for Ms. Keaner like it's Groundhog Day or something.

"Yeah, I can't *actually* do that yet, remember?" I call out before she closes her door.

"Hey, your solidity increased!" the secretary squeals with delight. "Boy, oh boy, that's big, dollface. That almost never happens in the first week—let alone the first day! Give yourself a pat on the back!"

This makes me feel all warm and fuzzy. After the day I've had, I can really use a pat on the back. Not that I would feel it, but still.

"Thanks," I say, and float over to the chair to hover like I've been doing all day.

Just as I'm about to pretend to sit, Ms. Keaner's door swings open again and out comes Georgia. This office must be like a weird ghost déjà vu wormhole or something. Doesn't Ms. Keaner know any other students?

"Thank you, Georgia," she says.

"It's my pleasure," Georgia replies with a big, fake smile.

We aren't able to exchange any words because Ms. Keaner is right there (and obviously we would only be exchanging rude ones), but I'm sure if they could measure the temperature of the energy between us, it would be swooping below freezing right about now (you know, 'cause ghost energy is super cold, get it?).

"Okay, Lucy, are you ready?" Ms. Keaner asks, grabbing her purse and shutting off her office light as Georgia practically skips out the door.

I nod.

"Great!" she says, and she picks up my backpack with all of my books that Colin left by her door. "It's time to get you settled in your new dorm room. You're actually not the only new student we'll have here this semester, after all, so you'll have a roommate."

Sweet!

I'm so relieved not to have to go through all of these firsts alone, I practically float away again.

"I think you'll find you two have a lot in common," Ms. Keaner remarks.

She leads me from the administration office, through the halls, and out the front doors of the school, which is the first time I've stepped foot outdoors since I became a ghost. The second I look out on Limbo, I'm so overwhelmed that I just hang in midair, dumfounded. The Limbo skyline looks like a video game! Everything—the houses, the stores, the cars—are draped in rainbow-colored holograms noting different percentages and types of energy. I feel like I've been dropped into a game of Candy Crush!

"This place is wild," I say, mostly to myself.

After about a ten-minute walk (or float, for me), we approach a large, eighteenth-century sprawling mansion-type building that says LIMBO CENTRAL MIDDLE SCHOOL: JANE AUSTEN COTTAGE. "This is where you will be living from now on," Ms. Keaner says. "It's one of my personal favorites among the dormitories. Jane is, of course, my favorite author. And a lovely person, too."

"You know Jane Austen?! She's a ghost?!" I cry out in shock. "*Pride and Prejudice* is my favorite classic novel!"

"Lucy, dear, everyone is a ghost. This is what happens to everyone after their lives are over. Hence the term *afterlife.*"

"So Jane Austen is actually here?" I ask as we make our

way through the larger-than-life-size front door and up the pretty, black-and-white marble staircase.

"No, no, she's not *here* here. She's off in the countryside in the south of Limbo. But she did donate a lot of time and energy to the school, so we created this dormitory in her honor."

"You're blowing my mind right now," I say, stunned.

"Well, then. Here we are," she says, stopping right outside a door that reads SOUTHAMPTON HALL, ROOM 312. "Are you ready to meet your roommate?"

"She's here already?"

"Yes, she arrived this afternoon. Her first day at Limbo Central will be tomorrow," Ms. Keaner replies, knocking once and then opening the door without waiting for a response.

I look straight ahead and I immediately think I'm looking in a mirror, which is odd, because I haven't seen one mirror since I've been here. But there I am—straight ahead: black leotard, pink tights, white tutu, pointe shoes.

"Um, I'm sorry, I'm confused," I say, turning to face Ms. Keaner. "What's happening?"

"Oh my god, LUCY LOU??" calls a high-pitched voice that seems to be coming from my very own doppelgänger. "Is this for real?"

Lucy Lou: a nickname given to me by one person and one person only.

"CECE?" I cry out, as my twin comes rushing at me. Cecily Vanderberg, my ballet-dancing frenemy.

Afterlife is just full of surprises, isn't it?

We hug tightly and it's the best feeling I've had in a long time. Must be all the extra energy in the room! In this moment, I'm so thankful for it.

"I can't believe you're here, Lou!" Cecily cries.

I laugh one of those really happy laughs. I can't remember the last time she called me Lou. It makes me feel all warm and fuzzy inside. When we met, Cecily said I was the least ballet-obsessed ballet dancer she'd ever met. While the other girls in class lived and breathed (and dreamed) tutus and toe shoes, I was skateboarding home from class or surfing with Felix. When everyone wanted to watch *Center Stage* for the billionth time, I was reading my book or watching the Pipeline Masters. The other girls thought I was weird, but Cecily said she loved how sure of myself I was.

But I should probably have mixed feelings, seeing her again now. Our friendship hasn't been the same since I hurt my ankle this past spring and she took my place as the lead in our company's recital. Truthfully, if the tables were turned, I'm sure I wouldn't have walked away from the chance to be center stage, either. But I think it was more about the fact that what happened made me realize our friendship wasn't as real as I thought it was. Our loyalty only went so far, but in the end, it was every girl for herself. Frenemies were about as close as we would get down there in the World of the Living.

But now, instead of having mixed feelings about seeing her standing before me, I'm so overwhelmed with happiness that I could cry.

That's when I notice that my stuff is covering the left side of the room. In fact, my whole side is like a mini remake of my room back home—including the fact that it looks like a cyclone hit it (just the way I like it!). I have the same gray-and-white-striped duvet cover on my bed, which is left unmade, like it always is back home, with my favorite sheets peeking out from underneath (white with orange crabs). I also have my same wooden dresser and bedside table, and even my lamp looks like the same wooden-and-white porcelain base with a white shade that I have at home. My dresser is covered with random knickknacks: a red clock, a copy of my favorite books, and a few *South Park* toys that Felix gave me. I even spot the skeleton key necklace with the purple teardrop stones that my parents gave me when I got the lead in the Marzipan dance in *The Nutcracker* last fall.

Cecily's side of the room, I notice next, is also the spitting image of *her* room back home, just as neat and tidy as only

Cecily could make it. One of our many differences. Her pink floral comforter lies perfectly, as if she's flattened it a hundred times, her clothes are already folded and put away (probably alphabetically by color), and her country-white dresser has only one thing on top of it: a pink music box.

"Okay, girls, I'm going to leave you to it. If you have any questions or trouble, just press the help button on your Tabulator," Ms. Keaner says, and points to the tablet-type hologram that is floating on the wall next to the door. "Lucy, obviously Colin doesn't live here, but, Cecily, your tutor does. At 6:30, she'll come to meet you and usher you to dinner in the main dining hall. I'll see you both tomorrow—I hope you have a good night."

Ms. Keaner leaves our room and it's just the two of us.

"This place is crazy," Cecily says, coming to sit down on my bed, and I sit down, too (really sit! I love being in this room, with its extra energy!), cross-legged up against the wall.

"When did you get here?" I ask.

"This afternoon."

"So . . . do you—"

"Nope, I don't remember anything."

"Me either. That's the first rule. You can't remember becoming a ghost, just what came before the crossover. That's what happens here."

"I'm so glad to see you," she says, and I can tell she means it. She gives me another hug, and I realize in that moment how sincerely happy I am to see her, too, and how determined I am to make sure that this time around our friendship is really real.

"Wherever *here* is . . . " she continues.

"Ooh! I can answer that," I say, excitedly. "Here is Limbo, and this is your *afterlife*," I say, matter-of-factly. "Cece, we basically get a do-over—a do-over of friendship, a do-over of middle school, a do-over of boys . . . give or take a few odd challenges. It's a lot like being alive, only it's like we've moved to . . . to England. So, like, they drive on the wrong side of the road, but at least they speak English."

"Huh," she says. "Fascinating."

I tell Cecily about everything that happened at school today: the solidity factor, the paranormal classes, the cliques, the Ghostcoming Dance-a-Thon, Mr. Perfect—aka Colin— and, of course, I warn her all about Georgia Sinclaire.

"I can't believe she threw a ball through your head!" Cecily cries out. "That's just so . . . so . . . cruel. Are you sure she meant it? Maybe it was just an accident? I can't believe anyone would be so mean."

"Cece, she told me to 'catch' and then called me 'useless.' There's no way it was an accident!"

Typical Cecily. So prim and proper, always looking for the good in people, and practically blind to the bad things in them. I guess that's part of the reason why it's hard to feel her loyalty as a friend sometimes. She is always so easily swayed by other people. Still, it's a new life—I mean, a new *afterlife*— which means it's time for a new *afterfriendship*!

I hadn't really thought of it until I started talking to her, but afterlife totally does give us a do-over!

"Okay, you're right, you're right, it's definitely suspicious," she agrees. "But if she's so bad, how is this dreamboat Colin dating her? It seems so wrong."

"UGH, tell me about it!" I cry out in frustration. "She must be, like, the best actress in the world when she's with him."

"Or maybe she's just super insecure and does mean things to cover it up, but she doesn't really mean them? Maybe Colin actually sees the real Georgia . . . " Cecily replies, hopefully.

"This is not a romantic comedy," I say, annoyed. "She threw balls at my head. BALLS AT MY HEAD!!"

"Yes, yes, balls at your head. Right. It's payback time," Cecily says, finally, triumphantly.

"There's only one way to fight fire, and that's with a big ol' hose full of H_2O."

"Uhm, I don't think that's the saying, actually," she says, sounding less sure.

"Yeah, I know the saying is to fight fire with *fire*, but that makes, like, zero sense."

"Good point. Let water rain!"

I smile. I can't wait till tomorrow. Safety in numbers!

KNOCK. KNOCK. KNOCK.

"Hello?" a voice calls from outside the door.

I look at the clock on my dresser and it says 6:25 PM. We've been talking for almost two hours! It's time for dinner, so that must be Cecily's tutor. I hope she's cool. We could really use a girlfriend to help show us the ropes.

"Coming!" Cecily calls, as she gets up to open the door.

"Hi, Cecily, it's so nice to meet you," says a voice from the other side of the doorway.

"Georgia!" I cry out. "What are *you* doing here?"

So, torturing me at school isn't enough—she has to make house calls, too?

"Georgia?" Cecily repeats, her eyes going wide.

"I'm going to be your tutor for the next week, Cecily," Georgia says sweetly (not *real* sweetly, *fake* sweetly, though I think I'm the only one who can hear the subtle difference). "Are you ready to go down to the dining hall?"

"You're going to be her *what*?" I ask, even though I hear her just fine and now everything makes perfect sense: why she was in Ms. Keaner's office this afternoon and why she seemed to skip off so happily. She knew something I didn't. And now she's here to rub it in my face.

"*You're* my tutor?" Cecily says.

"Yes! I'm Georgia Sinclaire. It's so nice to meet you."

"Hi, yeah, it's, uh, it's nice to meet you, too," Cecily says quietly.

"Well, I think we should head down now. Dinner is starting," Georgia says. She's being careful to keep her tone calm and sincere—sincere for her—and I can tell that she's already trying to win Cecily over. I'm so frustrated I could scream, but I know I need to try and keep my cool. "Your room is nice, by the way," Georgia continues, turning toward Cecily, as the two of them start walking down the hallway. I hang back to close the door. "I have that same exact music box in my room!" she squeals. "You'll have to come by and see it sometime."

"Sounds great," Cecily replies, turning back toward me to shrug with confusion.

Ooo. . . this girl is good.

BALLS THROUGH MY HEAD! I mouth back at Cecily. *THROUGH MY HEAD!*

"So, I hear your hands got a little slippery with the ball during gym class today?" Cecily says to Georgia, to my shock (and excitement!).

"Oh, uhm, well," she stumbles over her words. "You know how it is. I'm not very good at volleyball."

"Oh, really?" I reply. "How are you at water sports?"

And Cecily and I burst into hysterics.

Score one for the team.

Team Lucily!

THE
LIMBO CENTRAL
RULES

RULE #4:

Ghosts have powers, and we must learn
how to use them wisely and keep them
hidden from the World of the Living.

Chapter Four
Figure of Speech

It's Day 2 of my ghost life, and I can't wait for my fourth period to be over already. It's actually a really interesting class, and one that I desperately need to pay attention to: Beginner's Telekinesis. This is where we ghosts learn how to move physical matter with our energy, i.e., my one and only way to change the absurd outfit I'm forced to float around in, and do other things, like . . . *accidentally* stick chewing gum in Georgia Sinclaire's hair, for example.

I'm not actually going to do it. Jeez. I'm just saying I *could* once I've tackled the basic rules of shifting matter.

But I can't master the rules because I can't concentrate. Because after this period, we have lunch, and at lunch I get to talk to Colin *and* Cecily—who is on Day 1 of being a ghost and is probably feeling totally freaked out right now. I haven't seen her since breakfast this morning and I'm sure she has like a million stories about Georgia already and I can't wait to hear every last one of them.

I see Colin standing right outside the door to the class-room waiting to usher me and my book bag to lunch, and although under normal circumstances (normal being relative considering the last twenty-four hours of my afterlife) this would make me stupid with happiness, I can also see Georgia leaning up against him, whispering something in his ear. A huge wave of disappointment rushes over me.

"Lucy, you'll never move the pencil if you don't actually look at it," Mr. Chesterfield says, and I realize even though I think I'm being quite stealthy, I'm actually staring very inconspicuously at Colin and Georgia.

Hmph.

"Sorry, Mr. Chesterfield," I reply. I shake it off and try to focus one last time.

"The key is to try to break down the matter that stands between you and the item you are trying to affect," Mr. Chesterfield goes on to tell the class. "Whether you want to move it or change its color or physical makeup, it's all kind of the same thing, just a different output of energy."

There are a handful of students who are able to make their pencils float in midair, and one or two who have managed to change the color of theirs. Everyone is concentrating intently, and even I can feel the energy in the room shifting from place to place, like a warm summer breeze.

Right about now I wish I could output my energy to the hallway so I can hear what Colin and Georgia are talking about. I just really want to know what it is they actually have in common—*she* couldn't have possibly seen *Star Wars*, could she??

I wonder if the magical Tabulator has *Star Wars* . . .

"Lucy!" Mr. Chesterfield cries out, and then quickly follows this up with, "Watch out in the hallway!"

All of a sudden, about six pencils fall to the floor. None of these are mine. I realize that all of the energy I just outputted into internally freaking out about Georgia has actually lifted my pencil off my desk and sent it zooming out of the classroom and into the hallway, headed, it would seem, straight for Georgia's left butt cheek.

"Oh no!" I cry out, covering my eyes as the pencil shoots across the room.

Obviously I don't like Georgia, but it's not like I planned to spear her with a stick, either! They both look in my direction.

Nooo!

Things are already weird with Colin, thanks to me accidentally badmouthing his girlfriend. When he said good-bye to me yesterday, I could tell that he was a little less friendly. Not mean or anything, just, I don't know. Different.

"I'm so sorry," I say, finally opening my eyes. I float up and go over to the doorway. Luckily, they moved just in time and no one got speared. "I had no idea I was doing that—I really need to get control over my, uh, energy output, or whatever."

"Are you okay?" Colin asks Georgia, concerned.

"Yeah, I'm fine," she says sweetly. "Thanks."

"You do need to learn to control your energy," Colin says, now looking at me. I can't tell if he's angry or not. "We should start our tutoring sessions today after school."

"Perfect, yes," I say. "Sounds great."

Class ends a minute later and we head over to Cecily's Imprinting class to pick her up for lunch.

"So, Georgia," I say, trying to make conversation as we walk. "What were you stuck wearing when you crossed over?"

"Normal clothes," she answers, with a slight tone of "duh." "A pair of skinny jeans, a sequined T-shirt, ankle boots."

"She looked perfect when she got here, of course," Colin adds.

Ugh.

"Every guy at school was trying to talk to her, and every girl wanted to be her friend."

"You're crazy," Georgia says, gently hitting his arm in this flirty way, but smiling like she agrees.

I want to throw up.

"No, I'm not!" Colin continues. "She—"

"We're here!" I cry out happily, as we approach the doorway to Cecily's classroom. Anything to stop this conversation! Colin and Georgia look at me like I'm a five-year-old with no mental filter. Fantastic.

"Hey, guys," Cecily says from the doorway. "Is it lunchtime? I'm starving! Lou, what's wrong? You look annoyed."

Now Cecily's the one with no filter. I give her a look.

"What?" I reply, trying to sound cool. "I'm totally fine, don't know what you're talking about."

"Lou?" Colin repeats, intrigued.

"Yup. She'll always be Lou to me!" Cecily sings.

"It's so cool that you guys know each other already," Colin says. "Did you go to school together?"

"No," I answer. "We danced at the same studio, in case you couldn't tell by our beautiful, matching outfits."

"It all makes sense now!" he says, pretending to hit himself on the forehead, and I feel he's warming up to me again. "Well, it must be really nice to have a good friend here with you."

Cecily and I look at each other and smile. "It is," I reply.

Georgia nudges Cecily and begins to walk ahead, so Colin and I fall behind a bit.

"I'm sorry about yesterday, what I said about Georgia. I didn't know."

"It's okay," he says. "Really. She can be a handful sometimes. But when you get to know her, she's cool."

I don't want to agree or disagree, so I say nothing. Instead, I change the subject. "So, what are you going to teach me today?"

"Well, you've got your aim down pretty good. We can probably skip target practice," he says with a smirk.

"I said I was sorry! I didn't mean it. Promise."

"Right . . . " he says, not believing me, but in a playful way. He's still smiling, so I take this as a good sign. "I'm thinking we work on the basics: trying to touch the ground with your feet, for example. Maybe move up to walking and then sitting."

"Sweet," I say, excited. "Not pathetic in the least."

"Ha-ha. Well, I wouldn't worry. I'm pretty sure it's going to be easy for you," he says.

We get our food and sit down at their lunch table. Georgia introduces Cecily to the whole gang—which is helpful for me, since I didn't get officially introduced yesterday with all the Ghostcoming craziness (even though she purposely doesn't take the time to introduce *me* properly). I take mental notes as Georgia goes down the list.

"Listen up!" she yells across the long, rectangular table. "This is my new mentee, Cecily. She's awesome. Be nice to her or else!"

"And this is Lucy," Colin jumps in, "in case you didn't meet her yesterday."

"Right," Georgia says, her face pinched like she just ate a sour grape. "Cecily, this is the whole gang: That's Jonah the clown," she says, pointing to the burly, athletic kid who called me *Swan Lake* yesterday. I try to let this slide. "That's Marcus. He plays guitar in a band without a name with Jessie, who also plays guitar and sings"—she points to two other cute boys with sideswiped, shaggy hairdos and T-shirts with names of things I don't recognize: One says NIRVANA, and the other says THE RAMONES.

"We're just in between band names right now," Jessie says. "Which do you like better? Misty Mourning—but with a *u*, you know, like mourning for the dead, right?—or Man Without a Face?"

The whole table erupts in laughter. "Dude, we ruled out Man Without a Face last week," Colin says.

"I want to hear what the new ladies have to say about it," Jessie answers.

"Moving on!" Georgia continues, ignoring him. "This is my best friend in the whole world, Chloe," she says, pointing to her mean, blond sidekick. "That is Trey, Jonah's equally funny but less gross younger brother, and that's Mia, Trey's girlfriend."

"Nice to meet you," Trey says. "And I'm not *that* much younger. Less than a year," he directs at us. Then he turns to Jessie. "And Man Without a Face is the worst band name of all time. Seriously, dude, what are you thinking?"

"Trey is in *your* year," Georgia tells us. There's a snobbiness to her tone, like she thinks she's so much better than us because she's been dead longer. Since when is that something to brag about?

"Hi," Mia says cheerfully, moving closer to us. "I'm not just Trey's girlfriend. I'm actually my own individual person, imagine that?" I can tell she doesn't like Georgia any more than I do.

Good. We need all the teammates we can get!

"So, the rest of you are in seventh or eighth grade, then?" Cecily asks.

"Um, it doesn't really work like that here," Georgia answers. "We're placed in different class levels based on our skills and how long we've been here, but it's not like how school used to be. Limbo Central starts with Year One, then Year Two, and so on up, until you're ready to graduate and enter the real Ghost World."

"Oh," Cecily and I say at the same time.

"So, you and Colin are in Year Two together?" I ask her.

"Yes," she says, smirking, and taking Colin's hand into hers. "And we do everything else together, too."

Cecily shoots me a look. This is the first time today she has reacted negatively to something Georgia has done, in front of me, at least, which makes me breathe a little sigh of relief.

"Okay, so Misty Mourning it is, then?" Marcus asks the table loudly, and Jonah throws an apple at his head (but *he* catches it, unlike yours truly).

"How about An Apple a Day!" Jonah jokes.

"Mmmm . . . delicious," Marcus says, taking a bite out of the juicy red apple he just won. My mouth waters. I miss real fruit.

I barely have a chance to talk to Cecily about her day before lunch is over and it's time to get to our next class.

"I'll meet you out in front of the school at 2:45," Colin says. "Okay?"

"Sounds great, see you then!"

It's 2:45 and I'm waiting for Colin outside on the steps of the school. I'm so excited for my first lesson I can hardly stand! I mean, I can't *actually* stand anyway, but hopefully I will be able to once this lesson is over. Of course, I'm also looking forward to some alone time with Colin, but I'm more focused on learning a few real skills. I feel so helpless here, not being able to do anything on my own. And the countdown to Ghostcoming is only a week away, which doesn't leave me much time to figure out how to put something more attractive on for the dance-a-thon.

That is, if I even go. At this point, it's a toss-up.

"You ready?" Colin asks, appearing on the steps of the school as if out of the blue. "I have a surprise for you—you're going to be so stoked about where we're going."

"Ooh, I love surprises!" I say as we start moving.

We stop at the closest Limbo bus stop, and after a few minutes the bus comes and we hop on.

For a second I wonder why we can't just magically disappear and reappear where we need to, but I enjoy the bus ride more than I thought I would. It's exciting seeing Limbo like this, and Colin points out a lot of cool places that I can't imagine Ms. Keaner telling me about: Ghostbusters Theater, Clairvoyance Café (apparently if they can't guess what you want, it's on the house!), Cold Reads bookstore, Banchee's Bowl-o-Rama.

"We usually go there on the weekends. Actually, a bunch of us are going tomorrow night. You and Cecily should come."

"Sounds fun. Except for the fact that we won't be able to play."

"You can cheer us on from the sidelines," Colin replies.

"How did you know I've always wanted to be a cheerleader?" I joke.

"Guess I already know you better than you think."

He smiles at me and I smile back, and for a moment we're both quiet. I wonder if he's about to say something or do something, like reach out and hold my hand, even though I know that's totally crazy because a) he has a girlfriend, and b) even if he wants to hold my hand, at this point he physically can't and I can't hold his back. But nothing happens.

We ride in silence for the next ten minutes, and then he says, "Okay, close your eyes. We're getting off at this stop and I want it to be a surprise."

I close my eyes and follow the sound of his voice as I float off the bus and head in the direction he leads.

"You're sure I'm not going to get hit by a car or anything?" I ask, half-joking, half-serious.

"Don't worry, you can trust me. But if you did get hit by a car, it wouldn't be that hard to put you back together."

"Isn't that a happy thought."

I'm floating for a good five minutes before he finally announces that we've reached our destination.

"Okay, on the count of three, open your eyes. One, two, three."

I open them and stretched out before me is crystal clear blue water as far as the eye can see.

"You brought me to the beach?" I say, astounded. "I can't believe it. How did you know? I mean, *did* you know?" I ask, my words falling all over themselves.

"Cecily told Georgia at lunch that you guys are from California, and all about how much you love surfing and going to the beach. I thought it might . . . make you smile."

"This is the sweetest thing," I say, and I mean it.

"Well, I must confess, I *am* trying to trick you a little, too. I thought the hope of feeling the sand or the water again might make you work harder to get it right."

"Sneaky, sneaky," I joke. "I can't believe this exists here. I didn't think nature and weather was something that really happens in Limbo."

"Well, it doesn't really, not the way you're used to experiencing it. But since everything is just matter, we can create whatever we want. All we need are different levels of energy. There are ski slopes about ten minutes in the opposite direction."

"Do you ski?" I ask.

"I snowboard. Started when I was pretty young. Every year my family would take an insane vacation to this place called the Buccaneer Ski Lodge. I'd snowboard for, like, a week straight. Best week of my life every year, hands down."

"That sounds so fun!" I say. "I like to snowboard, too, although I didn't get to do it much where I was. I did skateboard, though."

"I've never met a girl skateboarder before," Colin tells me. "Given that you're standing here in a leotard, tutu, and ballet shoes, it's a little hard to believe you're into that other stuff."

"Well, believe it. It's funny. Ballet is definitely girly, but it's also incredibly hard," I answer. "You need a lot of strength, stamina, and discipline to dance. Just like any sport. Most guys don't think about that."

"True, I guess I never really have. Not until now, anyway."

"Have you ever surfed?" I ask.

"No, but I've always wanted to. We didn't live near the water."

"It's amazing. Like, you're scared for your life, but at the same time, you've never felt more alive."

"Maybe you can teach me once you can feel the water again?"

"It's a date," I say, without thinking.

"*What's* a date?" I hear a voice bark from behind me. I turn around and see Georgia, followed by Cecily, Jessie, and Marcus.

Of course.

"Hey," Colin calls out to Georgia. "You didn't tell me you were coming here, too."

"Well, when you told me your plan to do your lesson on the beach I knew that Cecily would, like, completely flip and want to come, too," Georgia said, coming around and standing next to Colin so they were both facing me, a united front against the enemy. "And when we told these guys we were coming, they said they were heading over to practice some songs, so here we are."

"Oh, right," Colin says, a little awkwardly. "Cool."

"So . . ." Georgia says, "*what's* a date?"

"Oh n-nothing," I sputter. "It's just a figure of speech."

"Figure of speech!" Jessie cries out. "That's it, folks! That's the winner! Our band will now forever be known as Figure of Speech."

"Seriously?!" Georgia barks, annoyed, but the rest of us just start laughing.

"Going once, going twice," Jessie continues, "sold, to the brunette in the tutu!"

THE
LIMBO CENTRAL
RULES

RULE #5:

Your first-week tutor will help you master the basics of being a ghost, such as learning how to walk, sit, and interact with your environment. The bonds between tutors and new students are special, and often last throughout the course of your time here at Limbo—and beyond! We urge you to get the most out of your one-on-one sessions. Your tutor is your after*lifeline*!

Chapter Five
Quicksand

When the awkwardness finally fades, Jessie and Marcus head down the beach to practice and Cecily and Georgia slip behind a cluster of giant rocks to work, leaving Colin and me alone again.

"Okay, the first thing you want to do is visualize your feet touching the ground," Colin says. "Think about each individual grain of sand pulling you down into it."

"That sounds like the beginning of a horror flick," I say.

He looks at me kind of funny. "You don't watch a lot of horror movies, do you?"

I laugh. "No, I don't. Actually, I hate horror movies. One night, when I was, like, eight, I couldn't sleep, so I came out of my room to find my mom, but she and my dad were watching this scary movie about a guy with a face full of burn scars and fingers made out of knives. It was terrifying! I stood at their door, peeking through the crack, and saw way more than

I should have, kind of like when you see an accident on the road and you know you shouldn't stare but you can't look away? Anyway, he haunted my dreams for years. Haven't been able to go near a horror movie since."

Why am I talking so much?!? Why? Why? Why??!

"Please tell me you know that stuff isn't real, right?"

"I didn't think ghosts were real, either, and yet, here we are."

"You're comparing life after death to some dude who has pizza-skin for a face and knives for fingers?" He laughs.

"When you say it like that it sounds ridiculous! But, I mean, it's not the *least* possible thing in the world," I argue.

"So what *is* the least possible thing in the world, then?"

I want to say, *Me ever understanding what it is you see in Georgia!*

But I don't.

Obviously.

Instead, I say, "Probably world peace."

"Wow, I think my soul just died."

"I'll be here all afternoon, folks!"

He laughs again, which makes me laugh. He has this one dimple on the left side of his face that comes out when he smiles; it's almost like his face knows that two would be too much, but one? One is killer.

"Okay, so, we were talking about visualizing," he says, all serious again.

"Yes, visualizing. Here I go."

I start to picture the sand pulling me down, trying to envision each grain like he said. First the grains are forming a line, almost like a chain to attach to my legs, but that starts to feel too jail-y so I lose that visual and instead picture them looking like little sand people holding hands, dancing in a conga line and kicking their little sand legs up like the Rockettes. Before I know it, I'm thinking about the Ghostcoming dance and whether or not Colin is going to go with Georgia, which, of course he is, and how much I like him and how unfair afterlife is, and the little sand people are all, "Yeah, that *is* unfair! Go get 'em, girl!" And then—

"Uhm, Lucy?" Colin asks.

"Yes, yeah, what's up?" I nervously break out of my internal crazy, trying to seem casual and not at all like I was just making sand people dance in my head.

"Look down."

I do as he says and am completely and totally horrified. Right there, in the sand below my feet, is the shape of a heart indented in the sand with the words *Go get 'em, girl!* etched into it. Like I had taken a stick and drawn it there! Except I didn't.

Uhm, aren't ghost powers supposed to be *cool*?

"I, uh, I . . . "

"I'm guessing that was you," he says with a smirk. "The last time *I* did that it said, 'Go get 'em, *dude*,' so that's how I know."

"Very funny."

Yes, this is truly embarrassing. And yes, I want to crawl so far into a hole right now that I would need a compass and a shovel to find my way out. But I have to admit, Colin has a real knack for making embarrassing things seem kind of . . . okay.

"The more you focus, the sooner you master standing. And the sooner you're good at standing, the sooner we can go surfing. Deal?" he says.

"Deal."

I focus on the sand once more, but this time I wipe my mind clear of anything emotional and simply try to connect the sand to my feet like two opposite sides of a magnet. As if there's an invisible bridge of atoms filling the space in between where I'm floating and where the sand sits. I wiggle my toes inside my shoes. I point my feet. I stand up straight and pull out of myself, stretching so far that I probably lengthen three inches. I think about surfing and how it feels to catch that wave. Feeling the water underneath the board—not actually touching it, but still connecting with it so closely you can feel its every shift and splash.

Suddenly, I feel a thud, like I've just crashed into a wall with my feet.

"You did it!" Colin cries out. "That was even faster than I thought it would be."

I look down and he's right. I am fully standing on the sand! I'm a ghost genius!

I kneel down to grab a handful of sand. At first I sense nothing but the air, but I wiggle my fingers and each time the sand disappears I dip down to fill my hand up again. Soon I start to feel the grains of sand falling through the spaces between my fingers—it feels hard and soft at the same time, and reminds me of Felix.

I feel a pinch of sadness.

"What are you thinking about?" Colin asks.

"Oh, I'm sorry," I say, even though I don't have anything to apologize for. "I was just thinking about my best friend, Felix. He's the one I used to go to the beach with all the time back home."

Colin comes closer to me and puts his hand on my shoulder. And I can actually feel it resting there. It's warm and comforting.

Just then I see a flash of black hair that looks an awful lot like Georgia's jet out from behind the rocks. What is she doing, spying on us? Why is she so paranoid and obsessed with hating me?! And where is Cecily?

"You must miss him, huh?" Colin asks, oblivious. It takes me a second to remember what we were talking about.

"Felix? Yeah, I do. A lot."

"Well, I know I'm not Felix, but if you give me a chance, I can be a pretty awesome friend, too."

There it was. That word. FRIEND. My heart drops into my stomach like a broken elevator car.

Sigh.

But I smile big and say, "I would love for us to be friends."

Then, all of a sudden, the sand beneath me starts to shift. It's a strange sensation, and I'm pretty sure I'm not making it happen. I try to lift my feet up, but it feels like something is pulling them back down.

"Are you trying to walk?" Colin asks, excitedly. "That's awesome, go for it!"

But I'm not trying to walk. The sand feels sticky, like I stepped in a huge wad of chewed gum, and I'm just trying to break free. Then the area around my feet forms a little tunnel and begins to pull me into it, like quicksand.

Exactly like quicksand.

"Lucy, what are you doing?" Colin says, assuming the problem is that my powers have gone bananas. "Just wipe your mind clean of everything and it will stop."

"I know I'm a beginner, but I swear, this isn't me!" I struggle to keep my balance as the ground sucks me in deeper and deeper. At least the times I've had things happen accidentally, I can point to something I'm thinking about—something intense and emotional—that can be the cause of my power. This time? I got nothin'.

"Are you sure?" Colin asks. "You think someone else is doing this to you?" He darts his head this way and that way, looking for a suspect.

I know Georgia is around the corner, but I can't accuse her of this. Not to Colin. Not after I already said awful things about her to his face the other day. We're finally on track. We're becoming friends. But I'm pretty sure she is the only logical explanation for why I'm being sucked into the ground right now.

"I really can't make it stop!" I cry.

My legs are almost entirely engulfed by this sand whirlpool, and I'm about to fall forward onto my face when Colin catches me and grabs me in his arms. We stare at each other for a moment, and the sandstorm settles a bit.

Maybe Georgia lost her focus. I try to peer over his shoulder past the rocks, but I can't see anyone.

"Are you okay?" he asks.

"I'm better now. Thanks for saving me."

I see another flash of black hair flying, and soon the quicksand is back at work pulling me down again. I wonder where Cecily is during all of this, if she can see Georgia doing it or if Georgia is just especially skilled at hiding her powers.

Colin tries to yank me up and out with all of his might. Aside from that brief moment in our room when Cecily and I hugged, this is the first time I've actually been able to interact with another ghost's body since I got here. It feels nice to hug someone again. Even if Georgia is pulling me into the underworld while it's happening.

"Oh no!" I hear Cecily yell. "Lucy, what's wrong? Are you okay?"

I look up and see Cecily peering down at me from above on the boardwalk. She descends the steps to the beach and rushes toward us. Just then, Georgia pops out from behind the giant rocks and follows Cecily. Almost immediately, the sand lets go of me, and Colin and I fall forward onto the ground. I'm smack dab on top of him, and even though I can't see Georgia's face, I have a pretty good idea what it looks like.

"What happened?" Georgia asks, pretending to be concerned. "Colin, are you okay?"

"I'm fine," he says, as we both get up and dust ourselves off. "But someone was messing with Lucy. Did you guys see anyone staring at us or lurking around here?"

"I just got back," Cecily says. "Georgia had me practicing floating all over the beach."

"I didn't see anyone," Georgia replies, a little too quickly. Then *she* nearly wipes out—her legs buckle and she falls to the sand on her knees.

"That was weird," Colin says, taking the words out of my mouth. "Are *you* okay?"

"I'm fine, just . . . lost my footing," Georgia says, but her face looks all pale, like she suddenly got very tired. "The sand is hard to stand on in heels."

I give Cecily a look and I can instantly tell she's thinking the same thing: Georgia did this to me. But neither one of us say anything. We'll have to debrief about this later on, but for now, it's best to just stay quiet. Besides, the magnitude of difference between what Georgia was hoping her little stunt would do (make me look stupid) and what her stunt *actually* did (cause Colin to grab me his arms and save me LIKE A PRINCE) is punishment enough, I think.

Gotta love karma.

"It's fine. Whoever it was is hopefully long gone by now," I say, looking Georgia straight in the eye. Just because I'm not going to blow up her spot in front of Colin doesn't mean I'm going to take it lying down. Or covered in sand, for that matter.

"You're probably right," Georgia says. "So, did you two get a lot done?"

"We're definitely making progress," Colin says proudly. "Look, she's standing! And she can touch. Watch—let's shake hands, Lucy."

Colin shakes my hand, and Georgia's face gets red again.

This girl, seriously. *Relax yo'self.*

It's not like he's giving me a massage, jeez. Anyway, after several seconds of demonstrating my amazing hand-shaking abilities, it's time to call it quits. I'm tired from being assaulted by Georgia's sand blender and I just want to lie down and gossip with Cecily.

"Well, I'm beat. Thanks for all your help today, Colin, but I think it's time for me to head back to the dorms and get some rest."

"Oh, sure," he says, and I can tell he's a little disappointed, which makes the butterflies in my stomach all happy again.

The four of us head back to the girls' dorm together, where Colin and the rest of us part ways. Cecily and I don't stick around to watch Colin and Georgia's good-bye. I'm already feeling queasy because of her stupid ghost powers!

Cece and I get to our room and crash onto our beds, exhausted.

"This ghost thing is *super* hard," she says. "I feel like a baby deer who can't figure out how to work its limbs."

"So you didn't manage to make anything happen during your session?"

"What session?" Cecily says. "She spent half of the time asking me question after question about you, and the other half peeking behind the rock to spy on you guys. That's when she wasn't sending me floating halfway across the beach."

"I'm sorry," I say. "I can teach you all the stuff Colin taught me. You'll pick it up in no time. I mean, you only had a week to learn my solo in the spring recital and you totally nailed it."

"I guess, but this is different. Ballet I can do, it's just a matter of learning the choreography. But this is like learning a whole new skill. What if I just can't catch on? What if I'm awful at it?"

"That won't happen. You'll get it, I promise. And I'll work with you every day until you do."

The room is quiet for a moment.

"Luce?"

"Yeah?"

"I never really said I was sorry."

"Sorry for what?"

"Sorry for taking your spot in the recital. But I am. Sorry. I know how much that part meant to you."

This apology is unexpected, and even though I haven't been wanting it, exactly, hearing it said out loud feels really good. I can't say that I actually felt betrayed when it happened. I mean, that's life, right? I got hurt. I couldn't dance. The show must go on, blah blah blah. But we never talked about it. She never acknowledged how messed up it all was, or how hurt I must have been—and I don't mean my ankle. So while I wasn't angry, I did pull away. I kind of just stopped trying. And, in a friendship, sometimes that's worse.

"Thanks," I say. "That means a lot to me, really." I leave it at that because I don't want to harp on it. Being in Limbo means I get a shot at a new beginning, and I don't want to spend my new beginning stuck in the past.

"So . . . what are we going to do about Georgia, then?" she asks me, smiling and turning over on her side to face me.

"I don't know yet," I say. "But she'll get hers. Those kinds of girls always do."

I don't want to just talk about me-me-me, but I can't help it—I have to ask, "So, what kind of stuff did she ask you about me, anyway?"

"You name it, she wanted to know it," Cecily says. "She asked all about ballet, and a lot about Felix. Who was this Felix guy? Was he your boyfriend? If not, did you have a boy-friend? Have you ever been out on a date or kissed? Like, on and on and *on* . . . I mean, I'm your best friend and *I* was get-ting sick of talking about you so much!"

"Isn't that the sweetest thing anyone's ever said to me," I joke. But the truth is, Cecily just called me her best friend for the first time, and that *is* the sweetest thing.

"I'm sorry! But it was getting seriously annoying."

"No, I get it! So . . . what did you tell her?"

"Not much. I tried to avoid answering whatever I could by asking her questions instead. It's surprisingly easy when you're dealing with a total egomaniac," she says, laughing. "Like, I told her Felix and you were just friends, and I said you were an über-talented dancer, which made smoke come out of her ears. Actual smoke! But when she started asking the stuff about boyfriends, I just redirected it. Like, *how long have you and Colin been dating?* And *was he your first kiss?* Yadda, yadda. People love talking about themselves."

"And what did she say? How long have they been together?"

"Three weeks."

"Solid."

"I knew you'd be pleased."

"I can't wrap my head around why girls like her are so popular, and how they always manage to suck the nice guys in. Because Colin is way too nice for her, and everyone knows it but him." I can feel myself getting worked up, but I don't care. It's so nice to talk to someone about all this!

"Well, maybe he's not as nice as you think he is," Cecily says, quietly. "I mean, if he can't see all the mean and shallow things that she does, then he's either really oblivious or he doesn't think they're as mean as we think they are."

"Maybe," I say, but I have trouble believing that's true.

"If he's really as cool as you say, and you guys really have a

74

connection, he'll smarten up about Georgia soon enough," Cecily adds.

"Thanks," I say, because I know she's trying to be sweet and cheer me up.

"Cece?"

"Yeah?"

"You're my best friend, too."

THE LIMBO CENTRAL RULES

RULE #6:

Ghosts start off weak, with very low states
of solidity, but strength increases daily.
Some ghosts get the majority of their
energy from food, while others harness their
own internal mental strength more easily.
Emotions can help you access your
strength, but they can also force you to
lose control of it just as easily.

Chapter Six
State of Solidity

It's crazy how easy it is to get ready to go anywhere when you can't change a single thing about the way you look. I can't put on a cute new outfit, I can't style my hair in that amazing beach wave 'do that takes hours to perfect but says, "I look like this without even trying!" I mean, I can't even put on a layer of clear lip-gloss!

The good news? It can't possibly get any *worse*. And if I can brave the Bowl-o-Rama like this on a Friday night and still manage to get in good with Colin and the rest of the gang, well, that's saying something.

"You ready?" Cecily asks me.

"Like I have a choice," I reply, throwing up my hands. "The wild, frizzy beast that is my hair will not be tamed, and I have to be okay with that."

"Your beast is a kitten compared to mine! My hair is so static-y I look like I've been electrocuted. Something about the energy here . . . and everything is more terrifying with red hair, you know that."

"I could argue with you, but I'd be lying. Then what kind of a friend would I be?" I joke.

"At least we have each other," she concludes.

"Solidarity, sister! Okay, we should get going. I want to get there before Georgia McScary comes knocking and we have to walk all the way over there with her pretending she didn't try to wipe me off the face of Limbo yesterday."

KNOCK. KNOCK.

"Looks like we're too late . . . " Cecily says.

But when I open the door, I'm pleasantly surprised to see More-than-Just-Trey's-Girlfriend Mia.

"Hey, are you guys heading over to Banchee's?" she asks.

"We are!" Cecily calls, zooming over to the door.

Mia throws her hands up and lets out a relieved groan. "Thank goodness! Not to be mean, but I really don't want to walk with Georgia and Chloe. I just . . . they kind of make my brain hurt."

"From the moment we met, I knew we'd be lifelong friends," I say, with a huge smile. "I mean, *afterlife*long friends. Whatever, you know what I mean. So. Shall we?"

As we make our way through the hallways, my Georgia radar is on high alert. I can't stop thinking about how evil she is! I wish I could just tell Colin that the whole sand blender thing was her fault, but I can't. I don't actually have any proof, and we all know how these things go. It will end up making me look way worse than it will make her look, and I'm so not falling for that.

Plus, she's probably going to look totally cute tonight. How can I even stand a chance against her with Colin? I mean, looks aren't everything. Her sparkling personality sure isn't winning her any good citizen awards, and I know I can talk witty circles around her in my sleep. Still, that little voice in my head that's making me feel bad about the way I look keeps getting louder and louder. I wish it would shut up, but I've spent my whole *life* hearing it and I'm pretty sure my *afterlife* won't be any different.

If only I could just not be wearing this leotard for a minute! *Argh.*

We manage to make it to the lobby and exit the dorm without running into her, and the second we get outside I breathe in deeply and let out a sigh of relief. I try to calm myself down, to wipe Georgia from my mind. And quiet down *my* mean girl voice. Afterlife is hard enough as it is without being my own worst enemy.

"Whoa, what just happened to your hair?" Mia exclaims, and she pulls a small mirror out of her purse. "It just totally flattened out."

I take a peek and sure enough, my hair looks like it's

just been dried and styled. Loose, beachy waves. Just the way I like it.

"I have no clue. I wasn't even thinking about my hair," I tell her, which is true.

"Well, somehow you managed to harness enough energy to make a dent in your hairdo," Mia says. "It looks great!"

"It really does," Cecily adds. "So much for solidarity, huh, *sister*?"

"I didn't even know I was doing it!" I cry.

"I know you're *trying* to make me feel better by saying that, but it's not working," Cecily says playfully. "You don't even need to concentrate to make yourself look like you just stepped out of backstage hair and makeup!"

"No makeup," I correct her. "I didn't do anything to my face."

"Yet."

"Yeah, yeah," I reply, but secretly I'm kind of proud of myself.

"It's like that time before the City Steps summer camp recital when we both tried to do that makeup technique we read about in *Center Stage* magazine?" Cecily says, turning to face Mia. "You're supposed to emphasize your cheekbones and forehead with straight lines of concealer, right? To make it stand out more from afar."

Cecily is starting to laugh now, and I can't help but join her.

"So we're both standing there, concealer in hand," she continues, "poring over the article, trying to follow every step, and we finish and look at each other and totally think we look awesome! We go out on stage thinking everyone is going to be lining up next show to get their makeup done by us. Well, of course, we get the pictures back a few days later and Lucy's makeup *did* look amazing on stage, while I looked like I was performing a scene out of *The Lion King*."

"You shouldn't have used my concealer. It was just a little too dark for your complexion, that's all," I reply. "Common rookie mistake."

"Yes, but notice how we were both rookies and yet I was the only one who looked like she was wearing safari camouflage."

"*That* is amazing," Mia says, laughing. "I wish I could see pictures!"

"Luckily, those didn't follow me here," Cecily says. "Unless they're somewhere hidden in my room and I haven't found them yet!"

"Oh, we are *so* looking for them when we get back," I add.

We turn the corner onto Death Row, and the view is exhilarating. Tons of kids are out on the boardwalk, and the beach is just to the right of all the action. The street is peppered with shops and restaurants, the bowling alley, Ghostbusters Theater, Cold Reads bookstore, Clairvoyance Café, Casper's Arcade, the Witch's Closet clothing store, and a bunch of other places with signs too far away for me to see clearly. We didn't have anything like this near where Cecily and I grew up in California. I mean, the beach was pretty close, but who had the time to go there, with ballet taking up every moment of my life! We had a movie theater, too, but that was it. This? IS AMAZING. We actually have a place to have fun and chill with friends. To go shopping. To get a coffee and read a great book. To go out on dates . . .

Assuming I ever actually get asked out on a date, which is still totally questionable. I've never been asked out before, so I have exactly ZERO knowledge about how it works. Cecily had a boyfriend this year. It only lasted for a few months, but still. She knows about all those firsts.

I've never even gotten a present from someone I liked. In fact, I've never even gotten so much as a note passed to me in class from someone I like. I mean, Felix always gave me something for my birthday, but that doesn't count. It was Felix, so . . . no warm, romantic fuzzies there.

Friendship fuzzies aren't the same.

"This place is awesome," I tell Mia. "You are so lucky! You

and Trey must spend every waking moment of your afterlife here together."

"It's cool, for sure, but I'm all about diversity," she says, as we make our way through the crowded street in the direction of Banchee's. "There are a ton of great hidden spots in Limbo. I'll have to give you a tour of all my secret gems. As long as you don't surrender them to the enemy?"

"It's a deal," I say. Cecily nods her head in agreement.

"While we're on the subject of enemies, before we step into the lioness's den," I begin, "maybe you can enlighten us about why Georgia's mission in death is to ruin my afterlife?"

"Okay, so here's what I know," Mia says. "Trey told me that a couple of hours before you crossed over, Ms. Keaner sent Colin a Holomail saying that he would be tutoring you. A Holomail is basically a hologram email with your details and a 3D image of you so he'd know who you were. He opened it in front of Georgia, so you just popped right out of the Tabulator while doing some superhuman ballet move where you basically jumped up to the sky, and his reaction was, what's the word . . . uncensored? I'm pretty sure his exact words were, 'Wow, she's amazing!' Trey said he had to physically pick Colin's jaw up off the ground."

"Oh my god, really? It, like, actually fell off?"

"What? No, it didn't, he didn't mean . . . he was just being dramatic."

"Oh, well, I don't know. Ghosts can do weird things," I say. "I saw some guy's head literally explode in the hallway the other day!"

"But that's, like, a trick. A jaw falling off is just bad engineering. Anyway, that's what happened. And obviously, Georgia didn't like that too much, so basically that's why she wants you dead. Again."

"He said, 'She's amazing'?" Cecily repeats. "Ouch. Sorry, it's just, well . . . I mean, ouch, right?"

"Yup," I agree. "If I were his girlfriend, total ouch. I would be just as annoyed as she is."

Because it's true. As horrible as she's been to me, I have to admit that's a 100 percent un-fun thing to hear your boyfriend say about another girl.

Boys are dumb. Even dead ones.

"Yeah, so she wasn't your biggest fan even before she met you," Mia continues.

"Well, that explains my frosty welcome in the admissions office, and everything since then, pretty much."

"She *should* be killing you with kindness," Cecily pipes in. "That's what I would be doing."

"Ha-ha, *killing* me. With kindness. Get it?"

"Oh my god, I'm a genius!" Cecily cries out.

"So wise, and yet, such crazy hair!"

"Very funny, Lou."

"Lou?" Mia asks, and I nod. "I like it," she says.

"Maybe if I really were a Lou, I wouldn't be dealing with such ghostly girl drama!"

"Well, brace yourself for more of it, 'cause we're going in," Mia announces. "Ready?"

We pull open the doors and go inside.

In my head, it's pitch-black and there's smoke everywhere and wind billowing around us, blowing our hair up like we're in a music video, and when we step out of the darkness and into the spotlight everyone stops what they're doing and stares. And Beyoncé's "Standing on the Sun" is playing in the background.

But what really happens is we just go inside and no one notices. Like, no one.

I see the gang in a lane to the right and we head over. I spy Georgia and Colin kind of off to the side, talking privately. As we get closer, it looks less like a romantic cuddle and more like an argument, and I immediately tense up and pray that it's not about me.

"Well, if it isn't the famous ghost who named our band," Jessie says, spotting us. "Glad you could join us. We're short one person for even teams."

"Happy to be of service," Mia says. "What team am I on?"

"Team Not-Gonna-Win," Jessie replies, smiling.

"Okay, so not yours, then?"

"You, Trey, Marcus, and Colin are the Beliebers, and Georgia, Chloe, Jonah, and I are the Minaj."

"Please tell me you're kidding."

While the players get situated, Cecily and I head over to the benches behind the lanes, where we can watch and gossip without being heard.

"Do you think they're fighting about what happened on the beach yesterday?" Cecily asks me.

"Why would they be fighting about that?"

"Because . . . I kind of said something to her today and I completely spaced on telling you. I'm sorry—it just slipped my mind!"

"What did you say?" I ask, excited and nervous.

"Well, I asked her what happened at the beach, if she saw anyone, but when I said it, I stared deeply into her eyes to let her know that I knew there wasn't really anyone else there."

"What did she say?"

"She said she didn't see anyone and that you probably just lost control of your powers and didn't know you were doing it, that she sees that happen all the time with new ghosts."

"Oh, please!" I cry out.

"I know! So then I said, if it *was* someone trying to mess with you, we'd figure out who did it. And then Colin showed up and said, 'Figure out who did what?' so I told him—"

"What do you mean, you told him?! You told him what?"

"I told him we were talking about who could have done that to you and nonchalantly mentioned that Georgia happened to be there all by herself for, like, a pretty long time, while I was floating all over the beach. And I said that whoever did it was someone who obviously has a lot of issues with you, then I asked him if he could think of anyone off the top of his head who might not like you so much, and Georgia's face went white. Like, she might have even lost some solidity, no joke. And then Colin looked at her like, 'Is there something you're not telling me?' I think he's onto her, I really do."

"Cece, you're the best, do you know that?" I say, sporting the biggest smile. "I can't believe you did that for me."

"Of course I did, you're my best friend. And you're the one who said this is our shot at a do-over, right? So I'm taking full advantage!"

Suddenly, I realize: I may have lost Felix in all this afterlife stuff, but I gained Cecily. Now I have all these questions I never asked her because of the whole recital thing, like what actually happened with her boyfriend, Parker, was she really sad, and did she have a friend to talk to when it was all happening. I want to tell her I'm sorry I didn't make it to her birthday party a few months ago, and that I'll never miss another birthday—or should I say deathday—again.

But all of a sudden, my body starts to feel tingly, and I lose my train of thought. It's like a current of electricity is rushing through it. I feel heavier, but in a good way, and the smooth, hard surface of the wooden bench we've been pretending to sit on reveals itself beneath me as the space between the wood and my legs vanishes.

I'm actually sitting!!! I'm not *pretending* to sit—I'm sitting!!

Like a *boss*.

"Whoa, look at you!" Cecily says.

"I know, right? I never thought I'd be this happy to sit again in my life!"

"Oh, yeah, that, too," she says, "but I mean, look at your body!"

I look.

"Oh my god, I'm solid again! I'm like a real live person, only dead. But alive. You know what I mean, I'm whole again!! I can't believe it!"

"That's amazing. You're advancing so quickly," Cecily

says, and I can tell she's getting anxious about her own progress, or lack thereof.

"You will, too, I promise. Tomorrow it's you and me, on
the beach. I'll teach you everything I know. Deal?"

"Deal."

"Strike!" Marcus calls out loudly, and we pause our conversation to watch him do a victory lap that's a cross between
the chicken dance and a baby breakdancing. It looks ridiculous, and we can't help but crack up.

Then Georgia's up, and I feel my face get hot. She's all
flirty walking down the lane with her ponytail swaying back
and forth, like she doesn't have a care in the world. Part of me
wants to have a really honest conversation with her and try to
peel back the layers of mean so we don't have to keep going on
like this for the rest of our afterlives, but the other part of me
wants to roll her into a ball and aim her down the lane at a set
of pins as fast and as hard as I can.

I'm staring intently at her ball, which is rolling straight
down the center of the lane, when it suddenly veers off to the
left abruptly.

"Oooh, gutterball!" Marcus calls out. "Sorry, Georgia,
better luck next time."

"Using powers is against the rules of the game,"
Georgia pouts.

"Come on, Georgie," Colin says, "are you really going to go there? No one is using powers to ruin your game."

"It was headed straight for the pins. Someone clearly interfered."

"Yeah, it *was* headed for the pins until it wasn't anymore," Colin continues. "That's bowling. It happens to all of us."

Georgia continues to sulk, but doesn't say anything else.

It's Colin's turn next. He looks over to where Cecily and I are sitting and gives me a little wave, and I'm pretty sure I start blushing like it's my job. But then he does a kind of double take, like something he saw made him flinch. I realize that he's probably shocked to see me in solid form—and sitting down—which is probably why he trips on his way down the lane and rolls his ball diagonally, straight toward the gutter. I keep my eye on the ball, and as I do, it starts slowly veering away from the gutter, back to the center of the lane, and at the last second rolls its way right through all twelve pins. *BAM!*

"Come on, tell me Marcus isn't using his powers to redirect the balls now!" Georgia calls out angrily.

"You can be a really sore loser, you know that?" Colin says, and goes back to the bench. "I don't feel like playing anymore."

"Looks like trouble in paradise," Cecily whispers to me.

"We should invite Colin out with us to go get ice cream or something. It's kind of boring just sitting here, anyway."

"Yeah, maybe," I say, but I'm not really focusing on what she's saying because I think I just discovered who's *actually* throwing this game.

Yours truly.

THE LIMBO CENTRAL RULES

RULE #7:

Once you become a ghost, you stay that age forever.

Chapter Seven
Afterlifelong Friends

On Saturday morning, Cecily and I head out of the dorm to explore the rest of Limbo—or begin exploring it, anyway. First stop is the Clairvoyance Café for breakfast. We're still not eating completely normally yet, but at this point I can down way more than a smoothie and I can't wait to get my hands on a—

"Blueberry muffin and a small hot chocolate with skim milk, right?" the girl behind the counter says, as she starts ringing me up.

"Uhm, yeah, how did you know that?" I ask, amazed.

She nonchalantly points to the sign hanging above the counter that reads: WELCOME TO THE CLAIRVOYANCE CAFÉ: IF WE CAN'T PREDICT YOUR ORDER, IT'S ON US!

Underneath the sign there's a little counter thingy that says: 103,624,512 CORRECT ORDERS AND COUNTING!

Mind. Blown.

"I guess this is where all the A-plus Telepathy students end up working," I say to Cecily, who has just been told she'll have a sesame bagel with cream cheese and a small soy latte.

She chuckles. "All I can say is, they really earn their tips here."

We get our orders and walk outside to sit out front so we can ghost watch.

"This is delish!" I say, biting into the side of my sweet, buttery breakfast treat. "I literally can't remember the last time I had a blueberry muffin. They're my fave."

"I had one a few weeks ago," Cecily says. "But it was fat free and gluten free and sugar free, and something else free . . . I can't remember."

"Taste free?" I suggest.

"Oh, it was definitely that. So, what are you going to show me today, Teach?"

"Well, I thought we'd just hang for a bit first, walk around, see the sights. Then we can head down to the beach and I'll work with you on how to stand. Sound like a plan?"

"Works for me. Hey, do you think Colin and Georgia are going to break up after what happened last night?"

"Who knows," I say, though I can't help but feel secretly giddy that she's wondering this, too.

After I realized I was the one who was fixing the bowling game—*accidentally*—Cecily and I gracefully took our leave.

We grabbed some ice cream on the way home and made it an early night. When we left the Bowl-o-Rama, Georgia and Colin were arguing in the corner. Again.

"I know she's horrible and all," I tell Cecily, "but I don't think I want to wish the pain of a breakup on anyone. Even her. It feels like that's the kind of thing karma would pay forward, only in a bad way. Is paying it backward a thing? Anyway, you know what I mean."

"Yeah, breakups are the worst."

"Did you have anyone to help you get through yours with Parker?"

"Kind of," Cecily says, but I can tell what she really means to say is no, she's just too nice to make me feel guilty.

I feel bad anyway, but I deserve to, so it's okay.

"You don't really feel like talking much when that kind of thing happens, anyway," she adds.

"What *did* happen with you two? Why did you break up?"

"Because ballet took up too much of my time and he didn't like being second best."

"Yeah, that makes sense. Kind of makes you wish he did something really dumb, though, so you could at least be mad at him, doesn't it?" I know I've never had a boyfriend before, but it seems like that would make it easier. Doesn't it?

"Totally."

"If it makes you feel any better, I'm sure he would've done something dumb eventually. Boys always do."

"Good point!" she says, with a smile, and her face brightens.

I look at her with utter seriousness, and then I say, "I want you to know that the next time a boy breaks your heart, I will one hundred percent absolutely, positively be there so you can cry pathetically on my shoulder and wipe your snot all over my shirt."

"I appreciate that," she replies, then licks the last bits of cream cheese off her fingers.

"Lou, if Colin and Georgia do break up, I think you should ask him to Ghostcoming."

"Have you lost your mind?!" I cry out.

"What?" she says innocently, like asking a boy out is no big deal. "I'm just saying, don't miss your opportunity. If it happens, his head will be all over the place, so you can't expect him to make the first move, and I think at least one of us should go to the dance with a boy."

"Can we please talk about something else? Anything else?"

"You need to loosen up a little," she says, thoughtfully. "If you can't talk to your best friend about this kind of thing, then you can't talk to anyone. Which means you're keeping all of your feelings bottled up like a balloon, and one day, you're just gonna pop."

"Is that your professional opinion, Doc?" I joke.

"Uhm, yes, yes it is. And if you don't listen to me, I'm going to be writing you a prescription for a whole bottle of I-told-you-so's soon."

"Funny. It's just . . . I would love to go with Colin, but what if I ask and he says no? What if he looks at me like I have twelve heads and laughs in my face?"

"Well, that depends. Do you actually plan on having twelve heads when you ask him? Because that will affect my answer."

"You're a regular comedian today, you know that?" I say. "What did they put in that latte of yours, funny pills?"

"Look, he's not going to laugh in your face. The worst that can happen is that he'll say no, but I'm sure he'll be nice about it."

"Like that makes it any less humiliating?"

"You either ask and have the possibility of getting what you want, or you don't, and you'll never know. Those are your options."

"How'd you get to be so wise?" I ask.

"It's the red hair," she jokes. "At least you have someone in mind who you could go with."

"I'm sure Jessie or Marcus would love to go with you," I say.

"Right, because the—what—three words we've exchanged since I've been here have really made a lasting impression."

"You still have a week. Starting Monday, you'll get your charm on and one of them will ask you for sure."

"Marcus *is* pretty cute," she says, kind of dreamy-like.

"Phew! If you said Jessie, we were about to have an intervention."

"Ha-ha, no, I'm good thanks. But, I'm not sure. He doesn't seem to be interested in getting to know me. Maybe I just won't go," she continues. "I mean, I can't even stand or sit yet. There's no way I'll be able to change my outfit by the dance on Saturday. At least you are learning how to do things! I bet by Saturday you'll be totally changed, while I'll still be stuck hovering over chairs in this silly costume."

"Don't say that. You'll get there."

"Really doesn't seem like I will."

"Why don't we head over to the beach now and get started? We can always explore later on."

"Whatever you say, Teach."

"Rise and shine!" Cecily sings in my ear. It's annoying how chipper she is first thing on a Monday morning.

"Five more minutes," I say, groggily.

After a whole weekend of working, I finally manage to help Cecily with standing—but it isn't easy. I have no idea why things are coming so much more smoothly for me than they are for her, but we can both feel the tension increasing. The moment her feet touched the ground I literally screamed.

And she's clearly excited to show off her new skills at school today.

"You're going to be late if you don't get up now," she warns. "Come on, don't you want to look all gorg for Colin? Show him all the tricks you learned over the weekend?"

"What tricks?" I say, throwing a pillow at her for good measure. "I managed to change the color of my tights exactly once, and I only did it because we were in the room and I had all that extra energy. I can't walk around like that at school or I'll get in trouble—you know the rules."

"Yeah, but the fact that you can do it in the room means that soon, you'll be able to do it on your own. Trust me, by Saturday you'll be wearing a prom dress!"

"You have too much faith in me," I say.

"Ye hath too little," she replies, Shakespeare style. She's got a lot of classes with the Doppelgängers. I think they're rubbing off on her.

When we get to school, we notice immediately that the vibe is, well, weird.

Everywhere we turn, people are whispering. Some big, juicy piece of gossip is circling around and everyone is feeding on it like a pack of zombies tearing into fresh meat.

Yikes.

"Morning!" Mia calls out to us, heading over to where we're standing. "Boy, oh, boy, did you miss a great aftershow on Friday."

"What do you mean?" I ask. "What happened?"

"Georgia versus Colin—big middleweight fight. By the end of the weekend, they called it quits. Hence, the gossip mill."

"We were wondering . . . " I say, a little in shock. "So what actually happened? What were they fighting about?"

"Colin was angry that she was being such a poor sport about the game and kept accusing her of lying about something that happened on the beach a few days ago. I don't know the details, but they are officially 'on a break.'"

"Now's your chance," Cecily whispers to me.

"Your chance to what?" Mia asks.

"Nothing. It doesn't matter," I say.

Just then the bell rings, and I'm safe for now. I walk off to first period, Famous Apparitions, without another word, mainly because I'm so stunned I can't formulate a cohesive sentence. Like I just ate ice cream way too fast and my head is angry at me.

Total brain freeze.

Class is, surprisingly, interesting enough to make me forget about the Colin and Georgia news for a hot minute. We're learning about the different famous apparitions who show themselves to people somewhat regularly in infamously haunted places.

"Remember," Ms. Roslyn says, "whatever age you cross over in is the age you will remain, so these apparitions always reappear looking the same—no older, no younger—exactly as they were when they passed on."

Hold up. Does this mean what I think it means?

Middle school FOREVER?

I can't fathom being in middle school for the rest of my afterlife. I've only been here a week and it's already stressing me out hardcore. Do I ask Colin to the Ghostcoming dance or don't I? Do I "accidentally" put gum in Georgia's hair or do I take the high road? (Kidding, kidding! Jeez . . .) But seriously, I can't be this way forever. I'll start hyperventilating or I'll explode or I'll start sweating profusely and get rushed to the nurse's office (not that that's happened before, or anything). And none of that is particularly appealing.

AHHHHHHHHHHHHHHHHHHHHHHHHH!

The rest of the day goes by without much excitement—except both Marcus and Jessie announce at lunch that they have secured dates to the dance. Cecily's face droops like she's five years old again and just dropped her freshly sprinkled ice cream cone on the ground. I know she was hoping that she would have the week to get to know Marcus and maybe then he would ask her. I try to give her hand a little squeeze under the lunch table, but without the energy in our room, I can't grab on to her. I feel awful, but I can't really get any alone time with her at lunch and I don't see her for the rest of the school day either. We have some classes together on Tuesdays and Thursdays, but Mondays, Wednesdays, and Fridays we're like ghosts passing in the night.

Before I know it the day is over, and it's time to meet Colin down by the beach for tutoring. We focus on walking, which sounds like it should be a piece of cake once you've mastered the art of standing—but it isn't. It's hard to explain, but it's kind of like being in an accident and needing to learn how to use your legs all over again. Floating comes way more naturally, and sure, that can be fun and all, but it's nice to feel grounded and in control.

"Just, uhm, try to remember that feeling you had when you first touched the ground," he says awkwardly, like he's distracted. "You know, and then, just extend it." He's probably thinking of Georgia, and I know off the bat that this lesson isn't going to get me anywhere.

Instead of working on walking, I work overtime to make him crack a smile. Right now, he needs that more than I need to walk.

"So, I gave myself a Mohawk in my room the other day," I tell him.

He chuckles. "You what?"

"You know, just to see if I could. Wanna know how I looked?"

"How did you look?" he asks, smiling.

"Incredible, obviously! So good, I'm gonna get my own doll. Ghostpunk Barbie. I can't believe you even had to ask."

"I don't know what I was thinking."

It's quiet again, and I'm anxious to fill the silence.

"Hey, let's go swimming!" I suggest. The water looks gorgeous and I'm tired of trying so hard to move my feet across the sand. "Maybe the swimming motions will help me learn how to walk?"

"You know what? That's actually a brilliant idea, as long as you can feel the water. It might really help you."

We jump in in our clothes, and at first I feel nothing. I think of our family vacation to Santa Cruz a few years ago, when my brother Sammy and I went swimming with the sea lions. Mom and Dad took, like, a million pictures and had one of them printed on iPhone cases for each of us, so we'd always remember it. The water brushes up against me and slowly I feel it start to stick and seep into my skin, the way a new sponge soaks up water the first time it gets wet. I feel freer than I've felt in a long time, and I start dunking under and swirling around, even doing somersaults under the water.

"Look at you and your fancy moves," he jokes.

"What can I say, I'm very talented."

"I knew that the moment I saw your photo pop out of my Tabulator."

I don't say anything, partially because I'm embarrassed, and partially because I don't know how to respond to that. Joking I can do, but once it turns too serious, I'm at a loss.

Instead, I nervously change the subject. "So, what are you going to be for Ghostcoming?"

And then I immediately regret it. Well, done, Lucy. Way to remind him that he just broke up with his girlfriend and now whatever famous couple they were going to be has hit a tiny snag.

"Well, I did know, but, Georgia and I are kind of on a break now, so . . . yeah."

"Right, I'm sorry. I heard about that. I just forgot."

Before it can get even more awkward, I decide to distract him by splashing a huge swirl of water directly in his face.

"Dude, what was that for?" he says, wiping his eyes. I can see his dimple, so I know he's not mad.

"I don't know, I just wondered, how can I pour even more salt onto this guy's wound, and then it came to me!"

"Thoughtful," he says, and splashes me back.

A water war erupts, and for about ten minutes, it's on. Then, without a word, we're both too exhausted to continue, so we just float there for a bit.

"I'll probably go anyway, you know, with the guys. I mean, I'm on the football team, so it will look bad if I don't."

"I didn't know you were on the team," I say, but I'm not even remotely surprised. I bet Georgia's a cheerleader.

Even in afterlife, some things are so predictable.

"Yeah, well, I do a lot of different things. Anyway, who knows, maybe it will be fun. Do you know what you're going to be?"

"Not a clue. But I can't enter the dance-a-thon by myself, anyway. Need to be in a couple."

"Right."

And then, I don't know what comes over me, but something about the breeze and the water and the marathon splash battle makes me say this:

"Or, we could go together."

It's dead quiet now. Like, if this were a movie, in about three seconds a shark would jump out of the water and eat me whole. *That's* how quiet it is.

What is WRONG with me?!

"It's okay, don't worry about it," I say, trying to backpedal my way out of this nightmare.

"No, it's just that . . . "

"I get it, it's fine."

"I'm just not sure where things stand right now, that's all," he says. And I know he's being honest. "Can I think about it and get back to you, once I know what's what?"

"Yeah, sure. No problem," I say. I'm suddenly freezing cold and anxious to get out of the water. "I think I'm done."

"Okay."

We get out, and since we didn't plan on going swimming, we have no towels or changes of clothes, and creating them would be super exhausting and time consuming—for Colin, of course. Since I can't do anything even remotely like that yet. Instead, we head back toward the dorms dripping wet. On the one hand, it's cool that my body can actually feel and absorb the water now that I'm solid. On the other, I'm dripping wet. So, yeah. I'm pretty sure I'm also dripping with shame so thick it's leaving a slimy sludge behind me with every step I take.

On the up side, the swimming was a success, and when we start walking toward the bus stop I'm actually walking. At least I can flee the scene of the crime with, like, 10 percent of my dignity.

The other 90 percent? That's back in the ocean being eaten by sharks.

THE LIMBO CENTRAL RULES

RULE #8:

We here at Limbo Central take pride in how we conduct ourselves. This means we are courteous, kind, and mature at all times. If you have a problem with a fellow student, we suggest you take it up in a civilized and constructive manner. Otherwise, you will find yourself in the principal's office faster than you can say "ghost."

Chapter Eight
Game On

"I still can't believe you actually asked him," Cecily says on our way out of a double period of Paranormal Energy class and lab that we have together.

It's Tuesday morning and the shame of Monday afternoon's overconfidence is hanging above my head like an umbrella on a perfectly sunny day. It's like when you go to the dentist, and they shoot you up with Novocain so you can't feel your cheeks. And *because* you can't feel your cheeks, you go to town chewing on their insides (gross, but true), and it feels so good in the moment, but when the Novocain wears off you're all, "That was dumb. This hurts."

"You basically forced me to ask him!" I tell her.

"I encouraged it, yes, but I never thought you'd actually do it. I'm impressed!"

"Wonderful. Well, a lot of good it did me. He probably just didn't want to be mean, like you said, and is thinking about a nice way to turn me down as we speak. Oh, well, there goes my shot at the dance-a-thon."

"Just because he doesn't say yes—*if* he doesn't say yes—doesn't mean you can't find another partner and sign up for the dance-a-thon," Cecily says. "I mean, look at us! We're ballerinas—since when do we need boys to dance?"

"Good point," I reply, because it is one. "It's just sooooooo humiliating to go to your first school dance solo."

"Thanks a lot," Cecily says. "It's not like I have a date, either!"

"I'm sorry, I'm just anxious. I've managed to avoid Georgia till now, but there's no way she doesn't know I asked Colin to the dance and I'll bet you ten bucks P.E. is going to be a nightmare."

"You're going to have to face the music sooner or later."

"Later, please?"

Just then the bell rings.

"And . . . *there's* the music. Time to go," Cecily calls, walking away from me. "Good luck!"

I walk into P.E. and the energy in the room is so cold I actually shiver a little. Georgia has her eye on me from the second I enter, and I can feel her gaze following me around like a clingy puppy. No, more like a rabid dog.

Out for blood.

"Time to warm up, ladies," Coach Trellis says. "Ten laps around the gym. Ready? Go!"

We start running, and since I'm still getting the hang of it, my run is somewhere between a jog and a hop. I look insane, like I don't know the difference between the two movements. Georgia, who can literally run circles around me, keeps coming up behind me and slowing down to hang out back there, like she's auditioning to be my shadow. Girlfriend, I already have one. Move it along . . .

Every time she approaches I feel a little extra push forward, and I assume this is how ghosts shove one another.

Very mature. This is *so* against the rules!

Finally, I've had enough.

"So you got bored just using your words, huh? Now it's time for action, is that it?" I say, all revved up.

"Me? You're one to talk, Miss I-steal-other-girls'-boyfriends," she spits back.

"I haven't *stolen* anything," I reply, but her words cut deeper than I expected. I don't want to be that girl. I'm not that girl. But then again . . . am I? Maybe I got my signals crossed and she has every right to hate me?

"Don't try to pretend like you didn't ask Colin to the dance. I know you did."

"I'm not pretending. I was told you two had broken up," I

say, honestly. My heart is going a hundred beats per second as I wait for her to say the words I dread most.

"So what, you can't even wait a full twenty-four hours before stepping in? How ruthless can one person be, really?"

Every word-punch she throws is landing, and I'm about ready to forfeit. I don't like the way she's painting me. I suddenly feel heartless and cruel, and I'm neither one of those things. She's the one who's been acting like a bad dream I can't wake up from ever since I got here, and yet somehow she's managed to turn the tables on me and make me feel bad—about what? About asking a friend to a dance after I found out he and his girlfriend broke up?

"Are you or are you not broken up with Colin?" I say, trying to sound strong. "Because if you tell me you're still together, I'll apologize and back off. I promise."

"Okay, that's ten!" Coach Trellis calls out. "Time to split up into teams."

She separates us randomly, and this time Georgia and I are on opposite sides of the net.

A few times, I manage to stop the ball in midair, but then I don't have the skills to redirect it anywhere. So it just hangs there like someone pressed the pause button on the best part of the movie, and the play is disqualified. Then we have to start all over again. Georgia, being an expert in my inabilities, keeps throwing the ball straight at me, so the cycle continues.

Then, when I'm not looking, she serves the ball straight at my head and *BOOM*! It hits me. Because I'm more powerful and solid now, I can interact with objects—unlike my first day, when the ball just went through my head.

It's a hard hit, and I go down fast. Everyone gasps except Georgia and Chloe, who stand there staring with smirks on their faces. Coach Trellis comes running over.

"Are you okay?" she asks. "What happened here? Did anyone see what happened?"

The room is silent.

"Enough is enough," I say, standing up. "I'm reporting you."

"What are you, a journalist?" Georgia replies.

"Is that, like, a joke?" I ask, confused, rubbing my head. Because if it is, it's the worst joke ever.

"Someone tell me what happened, now!" Coach Trellis demands.

"Georgia here thinks it's acceptable to throw balls at people's heads," I reply.

"And Lucy thinks it's acceptable to ask other people's boyfriends to dances," she retorts.

Everyone in the room is now staring at me.

Why is this happening?!

"Okay, that's it. Both of you, to Ms. Tilly's office—now!"

Coach Trellis says, shooing us out of the gym. "I won't have these kinds of immature outbursts in my class."

"Now look what you've done," Georgia scoffs, as we drag our feet to the principal's office.

"Me?! You're unbelievable. You started this whole thing! And you still haven't even answered my question. Are you together or not?"

We walk in silence for a few more minutes. The longer she goes without answering, the angrier I get. How dare she make me feel bad about this when they aren't even together? I mean, why else would she evade the question—twice! So typical.

"Answer me, Georgia!" I bark, a little too loudly, as we make our way into the administration office waiting room.

"Girls, quiet, please," the secretary says. "Remain silent until Ms. Tilly is ready to see you."

We sit in angry silence for what feels like an eternity. I can't believe I've barely been here a week and I'm already in trouble. This is so not part of my do-over plan.

On the other hand, I literally NEVER got in trouble at Parker Reilly—not once. So . . . I guess I really am doing things differently this time around.

"Ladies, please step into my office," Ms. Tilly says, peering out into the waiting room through her open door. We go in and sit down in two armchairs facing her desk. "I don't know what you were fighting about—"

Georgia butts in, "It's all her fault! Ever—"

"Buh, buh, buh—that was not an invitation to tell me," Ms. Tilly continues, holding her pointer finger up like adults do when they're trying to look serious. "I do not want to know. I am not here to help you problem solve. That is what your guidance counselors are for, and I encourage you to take advantage of their knowledge to get to the bottom of this problem you are having. I am, however, here to tell you that violence and unwanted physical contact are not permitted at any time for any reason at Limbo. There are no exceptions to this rule. Is that understood?"

"Yes," I say, immediately.

"Yes," Georgia agrees, reluctantly.

"Now, who would like to tell me who threw the ball at whom? And before you speak, perhaps knowing that I already know the answer will help entice you to tell the truth."

After a moment of silence, Georgia mutters, "I threw the ball."

"Thank you very much for your honesty, Ms. Sinclaire," Ms. Tilly says. "Do you understand that no matter what the circumstance, using violence to express yourself is unacceptable?"

"Yes, I do."

"And do you apologize for your behavior?"

"Yes, I do."

"Then by all means, Ms. Sinclaire, please do so."

Georgia turns to face me. "I'm sorry for the way I behaved," she manages to squeeze out through clenched teeth.

"Excellent," Ms. Tilly trills. "Now, I can only imagine the insurmountable pressure you have been under as the chairperson of the Ghostcoming Dance committee, and I have therefore decided to chalk this lapse in judgment up to that and forego any punishment for the time being."

"What?" I screech before I can control myself.

"Ms. Chadwick, when you become the principal of Limbo Central, then you can have the honor of choosing how to discipline your students. But until that day comes, I think it's best that I remain in charge of that task. Don't you agree?"

I hate these kinds of questions because they aren't really questions at all.

"Yes, I agree," I say reluctantly.

"Wonderful!" she cheers. "Do we understand one another?"

"Yes," Georgia and I chant in unison.

"I'm so pleased. You can see yourselves out. Ms. Chadwick, please go to the infirmary to get checked out and lie down. Ms. Sinclaire, please proceed to your next class. And one more thing, Ms. Sinclaire—next time, I won't be so forgiving."

Back in the hallway, we walk side by side in silence, and for a moment I think the war is over.

Silly me.

"You better brace yourself, new girl," Georgia says, as she turns the corner toward what I assume is the direction of her fourth-period class. "Colin and I are going to dance circles around you at the dance-a-thon, and when we're crowned Ghostcoming king and queen, you'll wish you never died."

"Doesn't everyone kind of wish that?" I reply.

But without another word, she's gone. And I'm left feeling bitter. And unsettled. Maybe she and Colin really didn't break up? Maybe Colin and Georgia aren't quite sure where they stand, and I actually did try to steal someone else's boyfriend? Maybe Georgia has every reason to want to skewer me . . . I haven't seen or spoken to Colin all day, so honestly, anything is possible.

I go to the nurse's office to rest. My head is throbbing, and I can't tell if the cause is the ball Georgia threw at it, or if my heart is just trying to send my head a message. Either way? I'm damaged goods. Also, if I stay here I get to skip lunch with Georgia and Colin, so that's a BIG plus.

Two birds with one stone.

I head straight home after school ends and send a Holomail to Colin telling him I can't make our afternoon tutoring session. Georgia will probably find some way to turn my considerate gesture into a marriage proposal, but there's nothing

I can do about that, so I'm not going to waste any energy worrying about it.

I need all the energy I have for important things. Like eating.

I so cannot face him right now. I can't bear to hear him tell me he got back with Georgia, or ask me about our fight today. I would totally lose my cool. And that already kind of happened once today. Once a day is my limit.

When Cecily gets home, I tell her everything.

"So, what are you going to do about the dance-a-thon, then?" she asks me. "I mean, if they did get back together and he is going with her, are you still going to go?"

"Of course I'm going," I say, feeling newly empowered. "And you are, too. I'm sorry things didn't work out for you with Marcus, but we're going to enter this thing together. It's like you said this morning: We don't need boys to dance. We've been dancing on our own for years. We're better dance partners than any of these guys. And you and I? We're going to dance Georgia so far off the floor she'll need a map to find her way back."

"Welcome back, friend," Cecily says, with a smile.

We spend the rest of the afternoon hanging out in the room, and I practice changing our appearance for a few laughs. I know it doesn't count for much, since we can't be seen this way, but it feels really freeing to get out of these pointe shoes, even if it's only for a little while. Not to mention how killer I look in a leotard, tutu, motorcycle boots, and a leather jacket. And seeing Cecily in fishnet tights and a top hat? Well, that's just . . .

Priceless.

THE LIMBO CENTRAL RULES

RULE #9:

Getting involved in school sports and activities is the best way to acclimate yourself to afterlife. At Limbo Central, each student must participate in at least one club or team. We hope that you will consider every group carefully and choose the one that is best for you. You have exactly one month from your date of admission to sign up, so use your time wisely!

Chapter Nine
Let's Play Ball

It's Thursday afternoon, and school's just let out. Colin still hasn't said anything to me about whether he's:

a) Back together with Georgia
b) Going to crush me by turning my offer down
c) Going to the dance with *her* instead
   OR
d) All of the above!!!

It's perfectly fine that he's decided not to go with me—I'm over it. I just wish he'd actually *tell* me.

"You should totally do cheerleading as your required team," I hear Georgia tell Cecily as I approach her locker.

"I'll think about it," Cecily replies, to my surprise.

"We'll have so much fun together!" Georgia continues animatedly, until she sees my face. Then she completely clams up.

"Well, that's my cue," she says.

"Wait!" I say, before I can talk myself out of it. This cold war between us has reached frigid temperatures, and I'm done living afterlife in a freezer. "I'd really like to put this fight to rest. We don't have to be friends, but can we just be civil? I'm sorry I asked Colin to the dance, okay?" I offer her my hand to shake. Seems like the most official way to do this kind of thing.

"No, you're not," she says, coldly. "But you will be." Then she walks away.

"Wasn't that fun?" I say, rolling my eyes and leaning up against the lockers.

"Why did you apologize to her?" Cecily asks.

"Well, with you joining the cheerleading squad and all I figure making peace is the least I can do."

"Don't do that," Cecily says in a slightly irritated tone.

"Do what?"

"Don't get all judgey without even asking me what I want or hearing my side."

"Okay, I'm sorry. What's your side?"

"I like being cheerful. It's my thing! Your thing is being broody and sarcastic, my thing is being happy. Also, cheerleading is, like, the closest we can get to dancing here," she says.

"I think I just heard Balanchine roll over in his grave."

"Uhm, he's not in a grave, remember?" Cecily replies, smartly. "Because he's a ghost. Oh my god, OH MY GOD, Balanchine is a ghost! Field trip??"

"Keep your tights on, dancing queen. Don't you want to *at least* be eighty percent solid when you meet him?"

She looks down at her feet. I can see my joke landing on her like a jab to the jaw, but I'm powerless to stop it.

"I'm sorry," I say, immediately. "I didn't mean it like that."

"It's not my fault I'm so far behind you," she retorts. "I'm doing the best I can, and everyone knows you have the better tutor."

"Nothing is your fault! Everyone moves at different speeds. It took Colin two months to change his outfit! Two months. I'm not . . . I didn't mean anything by it, honest. It was just a joke. A stupid, insensitive joke. Please? I'm sorry."

"Okay," she says, coming back to herself. "So . . . do you wanna go on a field trip?"

"I'm guessing we won't have time to hunt him down and make it back before dinner."

"Party pooper," she says. "Joining the cheerleading squad would cheer you up!"

"If I join the cheerleading squad with Georgia McScary, I'll be a *dead* party pooper."

"You're already a dead party pooper."

"I mean dead, again, I'll be dead again. Translation? I'll pass."

"Suit yourself," she replies, but I can tell she's still thinking about joining. "Are you meeting Colin now?"

"No, he canceled. Something about one last football practice before the big game."

"Yay! Let's go browse the Dead Man's Treasure Chest for some costume ideas for the dance."

"What's the point? We can't wear any of them," I say.

"Yeah, but we still need a backstory, you know, when people ask us who we are. And we need to know what couple to sign up as for the dance-a-thon."

"I'm pretty sure we can just say we're two ballerinas and no one will care."

"But we have to be a *couple* from *literature*. And you know Georgia will care."

"Uhm, okay, so we'll be Odette and Odile from *Swan Lake*. Everyone called me *Swan Lake* on my first day here, anyway."

"They're not ballerinas in the book, they're swans!" she says, with genuine concern.

"Cece, I hate to burst your bubble, but no matter who we *say* we are, we're still gonna end up wearing the same exact thing we've been wearing since we got here. You know that, right?" I say.

"It's just, I keep hoping that by Saturday we'll magically be able to change, that's all," she admits, wistfully.

"Yeah, I know. But I don't think we should get our hopes up."

"Can we please go, anyway? I want to go look around. Pretty please???"

"Sure."

We open the front door to the Dead Man's Treasure Chest, and a talking parrot asks us to pay a cover charge of five dollars before letting us through. I've never had to pay to enter a store before, but everything in Limbo is an adventure, so Cecily and I don't bother to argue. Also, it's a talking parrot. So . . .

The inside of the store looks like a scene out of a pirate movie: wooden and creaky, staged perfectly to look super creepy and old. The owner comes out from behind a red, velvety curtain and is dressed like a fortune-teller, which shouldn't surprise me, based on everything I've seen in this place, but for some reason, it still does.

"Hello, girls," she says. "Looking for costume ideas for the Ghostcoming dance? We've got every costume idea you could possibly think of—and the instructions to go along with them—for just fifteen dollars each!"

"I guess we're not the only kids from Limbo Central who

had this thought, huh?" I say, rhetorically. "What do you mean instructions?"

"Well, we only sell the ideas and the instructions on how to make the costumes, love."

"I don't get it," Cecily says, just as confused as I am.

"Oh, I can see now," she says, looking us up and down. "You're still new."

Cecily is still floating her way through Limbo—and looking approximately 50 percent see-through.

The lady continues. "Well, when you reach your full strength, you'll be changing your own outfits and such—you know how it goes. So we don't sell actual costumes here. Seems pointless, since people make their own clothes out of thin energy! But we do sell ideas and instructions for costumes you can go home and create yourself."

"Oh, *that's* why you charge a fee at the door."

"Gotta make money somehow!" she says, with a chuckle. "But it's all about the instructions. Kids come in here all the time thinking they can see something and just re-create it like that!" and she snaps her fingers. "But it doesn't work like that, nuh-uh. This takes hard work and skill. Took me weeks to perfect some of these."

"Okay, well, mind if we just look around?" I ask.

"Of course, get your five bucks worth!" she says, and walks behind the counter.

We take a lap around the store, and this lady isn't kidding—she has just about every costume idea imaginable. There's your classic supernatural section: zombies, werewolves, vampires, witches, the whole cast of Twilight and Harry Potter; then there's the official pirate section, complete with Johnny Depp–style Captain Jack; which leads straight into the pop star section, with Lady Gaga, Miley Cyrus, Beyoncé, Ariana Grande, and Nicki Minaj among many others; next, we enter the classic princess/fairytale section, followed by the TV section, with Teenage Mutant Ninja Turtles, SpongeBob and Patrick, the cast of *Adventure Time*, and a host of others. Then there's the generic costume section, with things like peanut butter and jelly, mustard and ketchup, doctor, nurse, a lightbulb, and, like, a million others. And let's not forget the period costumes through the ages section, which spans the whole left side of the store, starting with the caveman and going in ten-year increments all the way up to today.

I thought this trip would cheer Cecily up, but as we finish our long lap around the store, she looks at me and says, "We're not gonna be able to dress up as anything, are we?"

"I don't think so," I say honestly, and I can see whatever hope she has left evaporating.

Cecily's spirit is fading fast.

No pun intended.

I don't want to give her false hope, but she's not so good with the whole bad-news thing. Me, I can shrug things like this off with a tasteless joke and a sarcastic temperament. But Cecily? She doesn't have an ounce of sarcasm in her body. Things are good until they're bad. And when they're bad, boy is she down in the dumps!

"It's always good to have a goal, though!" I add, trying to brighten her mood. "I think I have an idea—if we can manage to make some small tweaks to our outfits, that is. Altering our existing outfits should be easier than changing their makeup from scratch. At least, that's what Mr. Chesterfield says."

"Ooh, do tell!" she begs, a little perkier.

"Miss?" I call over to the fortune-teller. "I'd like to purchase two sets of instructions, please."

We cross Death Row onto the boardwalk and head down to the beach. Ever since Colin took me here for our first tutoring session, it's become my go-to place to practice and just relax. And yes, I admit, there may be the occasional daydream about Colin and me surfing together. And our boards kind of crash and we both fall into the water and then he swims after my board and brings it back to me . . .

Like a prince.

Anyway.

We get situated and Cecily practices walking while I see if I can make a dent in this outfit. I read and reread the instructions for my costume, like, a million times, but after two hours of concentrating, I'm still no closer than I was when I started. I guess I thought the instructions were going to explain to me *how* to do it, but really all they do is tell me what the costume should look like. I suppose they assume that most ghosts already know how. Which I don't.

Shocker.

I try to think about what was going on in my head when I managed to do some of the other things I can do, like when my solidity changed or when I was able to sit and walk. It's confusing because half of the time my emotions end up making me more powerful, and half of the time they totally destroy me—for example, by drawing hearts in the sand without my permission! It's like, when they get too negative, they throw me off and I lose control. I need to figure out a way to separate my positive feelings from my negative ones . . . I need to visualize what I want without visualizing what I don't want.

I close my eyes and try again, keeping my eye on the prize. Or prizes, in this order:

1. Making Cecily happy
2. Crushing this dance-a-thon

3. Looking cute after nine days of wearing the SAME THING!

"Hey, you just did something! Look!" Cecily calls out.

I look down and my once-white tutu now has panels of red tulle with black spades on them. The remaining white panels of tulle have red hearts.

"Sweet!" I say, excitedly. "Dude, you did, too—you're walking!"

"Oh my god, I am?!" Cecily squeals.

"What were you thinking about?" I ask.

"I don't know, I was just happy for you, I think."

"That's it," I tell her. "The key is pushing all the negative energy out and focusing on the positive while you're trying to make things happen. Anger and jealousy—anything negative—makes you lose control."

"That makes sense," she says, thinking. "Okay, so, I don't mean to be negative, but I'm starving!! Can we please leave and go get something to eat?"

"Lead the way!"

The morning of the Ghostcoming football game, Cecily wakes me up in a flurry of excitement.

"Look, look!" she screams. "I'm almost completely solid!"

"Whoa, yeah you are!" I say. "How did you do it?"

"I don't know. I mean, I just went to sleep thinking about how excited I am to be walking, and tried to visualize what I would look like if I were solid again. You know, thinking happy thoughts. And I guess I fell asleep thinking about it, because the next thing I know, I'm awake and looking like this!"

"That's great, Cece. I'm so happy for you!"

"One more day till the dance. We can do this, don't you think?"

"I think anything is possible," I say. "I mean, look at where we are!"

Around six that evening we head over to the football field for the opening ceremony, and grab seats next to Mia, Trey, Marcus, Jessie, and their other bandmates James, Trevor, and Miles. I don't know that much about football, but the ghost version seems slightly different from the one I'm familiar with. Some of the players are floating while some are on the ground running. Sometimes the ball gets thrown, while other times it gets magically lifted out of people's grasp and tossed halfway across the field in the opposite direction.

"I take it, from the look on your face, that you're a little confused?" Mia asks, smiling.

"Well, um, yeah," I confess.

"I can't really help you, because I don't understand much, either. But there are all these rules about when you can use your powers and when you can't. Like, if you're within a certain yard length, you can float and use your powers to get the ball back. Stuff like that."

"Please tell me I don't actually need to learn any of the rules?" I plead.

"You don't. Believe me."

"Phew!"

We spend the first half gabbing about how the rest of our first full week at Limbo has been, and we take this opportunity to ask Mia what the best clubs and sports are. Cecily and I both have to join something in the next three weeks.

"I'm on the track team," Mia tells us. "Oh, and I'm also on the school newspaper, the *Limbolater*."

"Limbo Central has a newspaper?" Cecily asks, and I'm just as surprised to hear it as she is.

"Yup. It comes every week on Friday morning to the Tabulator in your room. You didn't hear the incoming message this morning?"

"I guess we've been a little distracted," Cecily says.

"What do you think you want to do?" she asks us.

Cecily doesn't say anything, so I jump in. "Well, I've always really loved photography. Is there a photo club?"

"Nope. Ghost photography is tricky. But both the yearbook club and the newspaper need photographers. They had three last year and they all alternated between the two clubs. But one guy just left, so they're probably looking for at least one new person. Colin takes photos for both—you should ask him about it."

"Oh, Colin's into photography?" I ask, trying to sound nonchalant.

"He's really talented. He's always trying to get our editor to put in creepy, black-and-white abstract photos, and he gives them artsy names like *Empty Bridge* or *Fruit versus Man*, and our editor, Stacy, always says no. They, like, fight constantly. It's kind of amazing."

Just then, the Limbo Central cheerleaders come out and Cecily's eyes widen.

"Looks like someone just found *her* afterschool activity," Mia says, nodding at Cecily's expression.

"I tried to warn her against it, but she just won't listen!" I throw my hands up.

Mia sighs dramatically. "Kids!"

Cecily smiles, and then turns to Trey and says, "Parents! They don't understand anything."

Finally, the game is over, and none of us has any real idea what happened except that Limbo Central won—rah, rah!—and that puts everyone in a great mood to celebrate tomorrow.

Colin finds us after he's gotten changed. I see him coming from yards away, and I'm simultaneously dreading this moment and looking forward to it.

What is *wrong* with me??

"Good game," I say. "Congrats!"

"Thanks. Listen, I'm really sorry I never said anything to you about the dance after that day on the beach. And that Georgia and I got back together."

"That's okay," I say, because I'm supposed to say something.

"Really?"

"Well, I mean, no, not really," I reply, as this week's frustration rises up inside of me. "You should have had the courtesy to tell me you decided to go with Georgia, but it's fine. I'm not mad. Being honest from the start would have saved me a fight and a visit to the principal's office, that's all."

"I know," he says, his shoulders falling. "I guess I just wanted things to be different than they were, but in the end, I didn't have the guts to change them."

"I don't have any idea what that means, but okay," I reply.

"So . . . can we still be friends?" he asks, flashing me the Dimple.

"We can be friends." I offer up a smile. "Just as long as you know that the Ghostcoming Queen crown is coming home with me."

And I'm so not joking.

Not even a little bit.

THE LIMBO CENTRAL RULES

RULE #10:

At Limbo Central, we believe in the honor system. This means we trust that you have upheld all of the rules in the handbook and acted with maturity and respect for others during your time here, unless we are explicitly told otherwise. Should we believe that any of our rules have been disregarded or dishonored by any student, we have the right to take matters to our school disciplinary council.

Chapter Ten
Down the Rabbit Hole

"It's no use," Cecily says, and plops down on the sand in exasperation. "I'm not going tonight."

"Uhm, excuse me?!" I screech. "If I'm going, you're going."

"So don't go."

"I have to go! I've been working on this costume for, like, two days. Also, I basically challenged Georgia and Colin to a dance-off."

"Okay, so you go and I'll stay home."

"I'm not leaving you home alone. That's depressing."

"Then it suits my mood perfectly," she replies, and drops her head into her hands.

"Come on, Cece, don't be like that," I say, sitting down next to her in the warm, golden sand. "We're going to have so much fun tonight that we won't even care what we look like, I promise."

"But everyone else will—*especially* Georgia."

"Who cares? Who cares what Georgia thinks? Let's just go and have fun with everyone else and forget about her. Okay?"

"Okay . . . "

I decide to go back to the room to relax a little before the dance. My costume is pretty much set—I mean, it's about as good as it's going to get at this point. But Cecily stays a little longer to work on hers more. She's managed to turn her black leotard a very, very, very dark blue at best, but at least that's progress!

I drift off to sleep, but at some point the door slams shut and I shoot up out of bed like it's a school day and I slept through my alarm.

"What time is it? Have you been gone all afternoon?" I ask groggily.

"It's six, and yes, I have been. I wanted to see if I could get the blue any lighter."

"And . . . did you?" I ask, a little afraid. If she did and I'm supposed to be looking at it, we're in trouble.

"Yes."

"And . . . is that it?" I ask again, hesitantly.

"No, I didn't want everyone to see me in it, so I changed it back."

"Oh, good." I sigh, relieved. I don't really care about people seeing me, so I didn't bother to change my outfit before I left the beach. But Cecily, apparently, is banking on the element of surprise.

I start primping and perfecting my look—only things I know I can change on my own already—like smoothing out my hair and giving my cheeks and lips a little color, which I finally managed to figure out. Having perfected all that I can, I look in the mirror on the back of our front door. The results? One pair of black fishnet tights, one red-and-black tutu with alternating panels and patterns of red hearts and black spades, one black leotard with white stripes, one black collar with red hearts, one headband with a red heart sticking out of the top, and one pair of black pointe shoes.

We figure this is the only time when our pointe shoes may actually give us an advantage, and since Cecily hasn't managed to change hers yet, we both keep them on.

"You look so good! I've never seen a better Queen of Hearts in my life," Cecily says with admiration.

I can already tell she's getting cold feet about what she can make happen, which will automatically translate into colder feet about going to the dance. I know I'm going to have to work some rare magic to make her keep up her end of our deal. Nothing the Queen of Hearts can't handle . . .

"Let's see what you've got, Alice in Wonderland," I say excitedly. "Your rabbit hole awaits you . . . "

When I first got the idea for these costumes at the Dead Man's Treasure Chest, I knew they would be perfect for us. I mean, Alice falls down a rabbit hole and ends up in a world of

CRAZY—hello?! That's *literally* exactly what happened to both of us. One minute we're alive and normal, the next— *BOOM*! We fall through a hole in the earth and here we are, in a world of CRAZY.

Then there are the costumes: for one, both Alice and the Queen of Hearts wear poufy skirts, i.e., tutus! Alice has blond hair—okay, Cecily's red hair is, well, *red*, but it'll do in a pinch. And me? I managed to add some red highlights to my brown hair, so that works! It even goes with our personalities. Cecily is all happy and innocent, and willing to give everyone the benefit of the doubt. I'm all, "Off with their heads!" Just kidding.

Sort of.

Anyway, it's perfection and I'm pretty sure no one else will be showing up in the same outfits tonight.

"So, let's see it!" I say again.

"I need to go outside the room," she says, shyly. "The whole energy thing."

"Oh, right. Well, I can just turn it down on the Tabulator," I reply, heading toward the device to decipher it.

That's when I get an idea.

A horrible, frightfully disturbing, very bad idea.

What if I only *say* I'm turning down the energy in the room, but I don't really do anything to it? Then Cecily *thinks* she's making all these changes on her own! Okay, okay, it's against the rules. So yeah, that's one big, fat red flag. But, I mean, she's come so far already! Who am I to say for sure that she can't do it all on her own? She's getting stronger every day. I know she'll have a blast at the dance if I can just get her to forget about the way she looks and the things she can and can't do and just have fun. Let loose. As long as she doesn't go crazy with her costume, no one will suspect a thing . . .

Right?

Before I know it, I'm lying.

"Okay, we're good to go! Show me."

She starts to concentrate, and suddenly her black leotard turns lighter, transforming into a Dodger blue.

"That looks great!" I say. "Is this the color it was before?"

"Pretty much," she says. "But I'm not done."

Then she adds two white stripes to her leotard on each side, extending from her straps, like suspenders. "See, it's like her dress!"

"Totally!"

"I wish I could do more," she says. "If I could, I would give myself cap sleeves and change my tights and even give myself a headband. Maybe if I just concentrate really hard . . . "

"It's worth a try. You're doing great so far!"

Then something bad happens. Okay, I *do* something bad. It's my fault. But I can't help myself! She's trying so hard and I just want her to succeed so badly! So . . . I close my eyes and think about how happy she would be if she could make these changes. Then my mind wanders to how she's really had my back with Georgia, and even though she could have chosen to stay neutral or whatever, she's hasn't. Like, at all. And on top of that? She's even going to the dance for me. I mean, let's face it, she's been totally bummed out and hasn't wanted to go for days. But she's going because she doesn't want to let me down. That's a true friend.

I'm not exactly *trying* to change her outfit for her, but I'm not exactly *not trying* to, either. Before I know it, I'm turning her tights and pointe shoes white, giving her leotard blue cap sleeves, and tossing her a blue-and-white headband for a finishing touch.

Uh-oh.

"Oh my god, look at what just happened! Look at my outfit!" she screams. "I can't believe this! This isn't possible, is it?"

"Of course it is! All you needed to do was concentrate a little," I say, trying not to sound too surprised. "I told you everything was going to work out!"

Yikes.

Now I'm REALLY dead.

The whole walk over to the school I feel like I'm about to hurl. I can't believe I just did what I did. I'll be expelled! I'll be the shortest living ghost of all time! Everyone is going to know.

Aren't they? I mean, there's no way they're not going to know. What was I thinking???

Suddenly, I feel weak. Faint. I grab hold of Cecily's hand as I stumble a little, trying to catch my balance.

"Are you okay?" she asks, concerned. "What's the matter?"

"Uhm, I, uh, don't feel so good all of a sudden. It's my stomach."

"Lou, you're white as a ghost! I mean, you know what I mean."

I don't know what is happening to me but I'm losing steam—fast. I feel like a car with slashed tires. Energy is seeping out of my pores. Even sitting down feels like way more effort than it's worth at this point, and it takes all the strength I have left to keep from just falling to the ground. I rack my brain to try and think of any reason why this could be happening . . . anything that Colin may have told me over the last week about powers and overusing them or something?

Then it hits me.

It's in the Limbo Central Rules!! It says—explicitly—that using your powers on another ghost not only takes double the strength and power you need to alter yourself, but it also causes extreme exhaustion. EXTREME EXHAUSTION. That's why my legs have suddenly turned into two pieces of very overdone spaghetti. *And* why Georgia fell to the ground on the beach that day after she blended me into a sand smoothie!

Uuuuuuuggggggggghhhhhh.

How am I supposed to dance circles around Georgia when I don't even have the strength to walk TO THE DANCE?!?! Even if people don't assume foul play from Cecily's outfit, they'll know something's wrong the second I show up acting like I just had surgery to remove all of my bones.

"Lou, are you feeling okay? Can you still walk?"

"Yeah, I think. Just, slowly," I say. I really want to start floating again, but it will be too suspicious.

Because of my delicate state, it takes us way longer than it should to get to school, but we finally arrive and luckily there's enough excitement from the moment we enter that no one seems to be paying too much attention to me.

People have really gone all out on their costumes. We have ample time to gaze around the room while we stand on line to sign up for the dance-a-thon and get our number. Within moments, I spy Romeo and Juliet, Elizabeth and Mr. Darcy from *Pride and Prejudice*, Christopher Robin and Pooh from *The Adventures of Winnie the Pooh*, Edward and Bella from Twilight, Mia and Adam from *If I Stay*, and Fred and George Weasley from Harry Potter. By FAR my fave.

"Nicely done!" Mia says, spotting us on line. "The

Queen of Hearts and Alice—awesome! I *loved* Tim Burton's version of that story. But Tim Burton is basically, like, a god."

I can see Trey trailing a little behind her.

"I didn't even recognize you with your hair like that!" I say, staring at the spitting image of Hazel Grace Lancaster from *The Fault in Our Stars*. "And you even have the oxygen tubes and everything! Oh my god, it's perfect!!"

A limping Trey, aka Augustus Waters, sidles up next to her.

"Well, you guys look awesome," Cecily says.

Then I spy *him* across the room. Yup, he's Four.

From Divergent.

Which means, she-devil must be . . .

"Tris! She's Tris!" Chloe coos, as we approach the front of the line. "Isn't she, like, the most perfect Beatrice ever?"

Mia, Cecily, and I just nod and smile. Okay, okay, they smile. I just stand there waiting for this moment to be over.

"And you are?" Cecily asks Chloe.

"Duh, I'm Cinderella. Isn't it, like, so obvious?"

"I'm not into fairytales," Mia says unapologetically.

"So, who are you two, anyway?" Georgia says, coldly, to me and Cecily. "And where are your dates?"

"We came together," I say firmly. "Just me and her. Sign us up."

"That's not how it works. You have to be a couple."

"We are a couple," I reply. "We're the Queen of Hearts and Alice from *Alice's Adventures in Wonderland*. I know you know that. Now give us a number."

"I'm afraid I can't do that," she says, smirking.

"You should be afraid," I say, getting angry.

Then Mia steps in, bless her heart. "Technically, a couple means two. And here we have two people dancing together. See? One and two, i.e., a couple. The only part of the requirements you have any say on is whether or not they are from a work of literature, which, unless you're as ignorant about books as you are about people, you can clearly see they are. So, let's just drop this insanity right now. Give them a number."

Loving this girl!

Georgia's got nothing, but I can tell the wheels in her head are spinning fast. She's trying to think of another way to disqualify us.

"Hey, guys!" Colin calls out, appearing at my side as if by magic. "Lucy, Cecily, you look great! I can't believe you managed to change your outfits so quickly. You two are, like, the fastest, strongest ghosts we've had here in a long time."

"You know, Colin, you're right," Georgia says, but not in that "way to go!" voice that Colin has. Something's a-brewin' in her mind.

And I think I know exactly what it is.

"Colin, how long did it take you to change your outfit?" she asks.

"Two months."

"And you, Mia?"

"A month."

"And you, Chloe?"

"Five weeks."

She goes on to ask Trey, and a few other people standing on line, and everyone's answer has one damning thing in common: Each one is significantly longer than a little over a week.

"Curious," Georgia says.

But before she can continue, the rest of the crew appears: Jonah, dressed like Prince Charming to Chloe's Cinderella; Jessie and his date, dressed like Peeta and Katniss from The Hunger Games; and Marcus and his date, dressed like Harry Potter and Ginny Weasley.

I know this is going to sting Cecily because she has natural red hair and would have literally been the perfect Ginny to Marcus's Harry.

Quickly, I whisper in Cecily's ear, "Me? I've always been partial to Ron and Hermione. They're *obviously* the cooler couple."

She smiles. "Obviously! Hey, are you feeling any better?"

"What's the matter, Lucy?" Georgia pipes in. "Feeling tired?"

"No, I'm fine."

But this ship has already sailed, and we're in for some seriously stormy weather.

"Oh, Ms. Roslyn?" Georgia calls out to the first teacher who walks by us. "Can you please ask Ms. Tilly to come over to the sign-up table? Lucy Chadwick and Cecily Vanderberg have broken the rules of Limbo Central."

Ahhhhhhhh!

Yup, that's the sound of us falling all the way down the rabbit hole.

THE
LIMBO CENTRAL
RULES

RULE #11:

Being a ghost and having to learn a whole new way of afterlife can feel lonely at times. You will miss your past life. This is natural. Know that the most important tool any ghost can possess is the power of positivity, and positivity starts by growing and maintaining true friendships. Believing in the power of love and goodness will serve you for the rest of your afterlife.

Chapter Eleven
Moment of Truth

"Georgia, what are you saying?" Colin shouts angrily. "Don't do this, it's not fair."

But it's too late. Ms. Roslyn has already left to fetch Ms. Tilly.

"I'm just being honest," Georgia says. "There's no way they could have done this in a week's time."

"I know you're jealous, but this is going too far," Colin continues. "I promised I'd go with you tonight if you stopped all this crazy mean-girl stuff, and here I am. You need to keep your promise, too."

Aha!

Georgia said she'd back off of me if he went to the dance with her, and he agreed. For me. Which means he really did want to come with me after all . . . not that that's what's important now. Because it SO isn't.

"That's not what this is, Colin," Georgia goes on. "Lucy is more powerful than most of us, maybe, but there's no way

Cecily did this on her own. I know—I'm her tutor. She was still half see-through, like, a day ago."

Everyone is quiet then. I know they're all secretly processing what Georgia said and wondering if it's true. I feel like I just swallowed a lump of coal. I can't let Cecily go down for my mistake. What kind of a friend would I be if I did?

"I worked really hard on this outfit," Cecily says. "I'm as surprised as you are, but I did it all by myself. I swear."

"I was there," I say. Technically, that's true.

"Yeah, well, we'll see. Won't we?" Georgia answers.

"Girls, what seems to be the problem?" Ms. Tilly says, appearing by Georgia's side behind the table. "I was told there was some kind of breach of the honor system?"

"Cecily started at Limbo only a little over a week ago, Ms. Tilly," Georgia begins, "and I am her tutor. There's no way she possesses the strength or skill at this point to be able to change her appearance on her own. Someone interfered, and that someone is Lucy Chadwick."

"This is very serious, indeed," Ms. Tilly says. "Ms. Vanderberg, what is your response to this?"

"I don't know why I suddenly started gaining strength over the last few days, but I have. I did this on my own. Lucy didn't do anything."

Then Ms. Tilly turns to me. "Ms. Chadwick, do you stand by Ms. Vanderberg?"

What an oddly worded question . . . I could just come out with the truth here and now. But that would destroy Cecily. Like, into a million little pieces. And she'd hate me forever. Or, I could answer Ms. Tilly's question—the *exact* question that she asked. Do I stand by my best friend?

"Absolutely," I say.

But the word feels unsettling down in my gut. This is the second time I've lied today, and all of my lies are bubbling around inside me like a boiling stew, getting ready to rise up and blow my lid off. This is not the kind of person I am. This is not the kind of person I want to be.

"Well then, there is only one way to settle this," Ms. Tilly says.

We all stare at her in silence, waiting with baited breath to hear that one way . . . What if Ms. Tilly tries to expel Cecily? I can't let that happen. So much for my do-over, huh? I couldn't even make it two weeks without getting myself into some serious trouble and mucking everything up for everyone.

"At Limbo Central we practice the Honor System," Ms. Tilly begins. "We expect you to be honest with us, and if that honesty is challenged, we must give you every opportunity to prove that your word is true before punishing you for its falseness. Cecily, please come with me. If you can demonstrate that you have the power and skill to alter your appearance here and now, we will forget this matter ever happened."

I squeeze Cecily's hand and whisper, "Good luck! Just remember: Think positive thoughts. Push all the negativity out and think of things that make you happy. Think of people you love. I'll be right there when you come out. I know you can do this. I believe in you."

As Cecily and Ms. Tilly walk away, I hang back for a moment to get some facetime with Georgia. There's no way I'm letting Cecily go down, but before I do what I have to do, Georgia's going to learn a very important lesson.

What goes around comes around.

"Hey, Georgia?" I say calmly, and pull her aside. "I know Cecily is gonna be fine in there, but just in case she cracks under pressure, I have a little surprise for you: I know it was you manipulating the sand to pull me down on the beach that day. I saw you spying on us, and I know you dropped to the ground afterward because you were so tired from breaking all those Limbo Central rules you pretend to care about so much. And Cecily knows it, too. And after everything you've pulled, it won't take long to convince Colin that it was you—that is, if he doesn't already know it. So, if Cecily gets in any trouble for this, I'm telling Ms. Tilly everything—and you're going down, too. Remember what she said after what you did in P.E.? Next time she won't be so forgiving."

Then, before she can say a word (and I'm certain she has about a thousand on the tip of her tongue), I turn away. I need to get to the administration building, like, now. I only stayed back to talk to Georgia for a minute or two, so I figure catching up to Ms. Tilly and Cecily won't be a problem. Except for one minor detail: I have spaghetti for legs.

Uh-oh.

How could I be so forgetful? How did I just completely space on the fact that I can't walk, let alone run?! Poor Cecily. I'm the worst friend. I was so upset with her about taking my spot in the recital and *that* wasn't even her fault! But this *is* my fault. It's all my fault. And I didn't even have the courtesy to tell her I was doing it. I didn't give her a choice. I didn't ask her if she wanted to break the rules. I just did it, and now she's going to get punished.

Then it hits me. I didn't *ask* her. She didn't know! Which means that *she* didn't break the rules—only I did! So the only person who has to go down for this is me. If I can just get there already to come clean, everything is going to be fine.

At least for her.

Ten minutes later, I drag my sorry, boneless body to the door of Ms. Tilly's office and knock.

"Just one moment!" I hear Ms. Tilly call out.

But I can't wait another moment. I need to tell her the truth, now. So I burst in.

"Ms. Chadwick, didn't you hear me? I said *one moment*. We are just finishing up in here, please close the door."

I look over at Cecily and her face is beaming like she just got an all-expenses-paid trip to Universal Studios.

Then I take in her costume. Her tights now have blue-and-white stripes, and her skirt has a new blue apron-like top layer with a picture of a bunny rabbit on it.

She did it. She harnessed the energy around her and she actually pulled it off!

"Ms. Chadwick, please close the door," Ms. Tilly says again, this time a little more commanding.

"Oh, yes, of course, I'm sorry."

I step away as gracefully as I can so as not to arouse suspicion and go sit down in one of the armchairs in her waiting room. By some miracle, Cecily has proven herself and gotten me out of this horrible bind.

I owe her my afterlife.

"Thanks, Ms. Tilly," Cecily says on her way out of the office.

"You did it!" I squeal, and get up to give Cecily a hug, but teeter a little in the process.

"Are you still feeling sick?" she asks, concerned.

How can she be worried about *me* right now?!

"I'm fine," I say. "Let's go celebrate YOU!"

As we walk from the administration building back to the auditorium, I decide to tell Cecily what I've done. I don't want to start our new afterlife friendship with lies. Being honest is the only way to be a good friend. And if she's mad at me, well, that's okay because I deserve it.

And so I tell her.

"That's the truth," I confess. "And I'm really, really sorry I did it. I never wanted to put you in danger. If you tell me you want me to go in there and tell Ms. Tilly everything, I will. Just to prove how sorry I am."

After endless minutes of silence, she finally asks, "Why did you do it?"

"I wanted you to have fun. I wanted you to feel good about yourself and what you've accomplished. I knew you were sad about not advancing as quickly as me, and I knew you were bummed about Marcus. I was worried that you would decide not to go and bail at the last minute, and miss out on something really important. And fun."

A few more seconds float by. They feel like hours.

"Okay," she says, finally.

"Okay, what?"

"Just, okay."

"Aren't you mad? Don't you hate me? Don't you even want to yell at me a little?" I cry out, in disbelief.

"Not really. I mean, not unless you want me to."

"Come on, Cece. Say something else, anything else."

"Okay, then I wish you hadn't done it, but I understand that you were just trying to help me because you wanted me to be happy. And I appreciate the thought behind it. But next time you want to break the rules with me, ask me first, okay?"

"Believe me, I won't be breaking the rules ever again!" I say.

"Oh, really?"

"Fine, well, for a really, really, really long time then. At least." Then I switch subjects. "So . . . how did you do it, in Ms. Tilly's office? How did you make it happen?"

"I thought a lot about you and what you said before I left. About focusing on positive thinking and getting rid of all the negativity. So I erased Georgia from my head, and I thought about how close we've become in the last two weeks, and how different it already feels from what it was like before. I wanted you to be proud of me—I wanted to give you a real reason to believe in me the way you said you did."

"Cece, I'm so, so glad that you showed Ms. Tilly and that everything worked out for you—and for me—tonight. But, you know, even if you hadn't been able to pull it off? I would still believe in you. I'll always have your back. Always."

"I know," she says. "And I think that's why it worked."

I reach out and hug her—a real hug.

Nailed it!

"Now, we have to get you some food—and fast," Cecily says. "You can't enter the dance-a-thon like this."

We head over to the vending machines on the third floor of the main building and buy as many snacks as we can afford with the ten bucks we stuffed in our tutus. After one package of crackers and cheese, one bag of pretzels, one bag of sour cream and onion potato chips, one granola bar, and two Twix bars, I'm feeling significantly more energized.

And like I might puke.

Whoops!

"Are you feeling better now?" Cecily asks.

"Define 'better.'"

"Can you dance?"

"I think so," I say, stuffing a few extra snacks in my leotard just in case I need more later. "But there's also a very good chance I'll vomit all over you in the process."

"One problem at a time, Lou. One problem at a time."

We re-enter the auditorium about forty-five minutes after we left, and all eyes are on us. Bad news really does travel fast. Even though I know I'm not *supposed* to be enjoying this, I have to admit it's a little cool being the center of attention.

Right now, we hold the element of surprise in our hands. We are the gossip.

"Oh my god, you're enjoying this, aren't you?" Cecily says playfully as we walk through the wide-eyed crowd.

"So are you!" I say back. "Besides, have you ever met a dancer who didn't like being in the spotlight?"

"Fair enough."

We march back up to the dance-a-thon sign-in desk and there are Georgia and Chloe, just where we left them. So is the rest of the gang.

Only, Georgia looks significantly smaller now.

Maybe it's just that she isn't letting her loud mouth run amuck anymore, but something definitely feels different.

"What's the matter, Georgia? Cat got your tongue?" I ask.

Silence follows. She's clearly uncomfortable and knows she's about to get served. That's what happens when you play with fire.

I'm about to tell her what's what, when to my surprise, Cecily begins to speak.

"Thanks for throwing me under the bus, all for a boy and a chance to get rid of Lucy. I thought tutors and mentees were supposed to have a special bond, or whatever. Maybe the reason you thought I couldn't possibly have the strength to do this on my own is because you have absolutely no idea what it means to have a true friend in your corner helping you and believing in you. If I had relied on your tutoring, yeah, I never would have been able to do any of this. Because you're the worst tutor ever. Lucy was the one who helped me. Every day she taught me what she learned from Colin and on her own. If you spent more time being a decent person and less time obsessing over Lucy, maybe you wouldn't have to work so hard to get people to tolerate you. One day you'll realize how lonely it is being a person full of jealousy and anger, and maybe then, you'll start to change how you behave. Until then, I really don't want to have anything to do with you. Now, give us a number for the dance-a-thon—it's time to show you what we can *really* do."

Jaws on the ground.

No, not literally, but they could be and it would be totally understandable. Cecily just served it high, hard, and so far over the net, the play was over before it even began. *OUCH!*

"Uh, that was insane," I say to her, after we get our numbers and move away from the table.

I am already starting to feel stronger after the seven-course vending machine meal I ate, but watching Cecily stand up for herself like that and tell Georgia off just lifts my spirit even more.

I'm *so* ready to kill her in this dance-a-thon.

No pun intended. Times two.

"Girl, I'm impressed," Mia says to Cecily, coming over to us with the rest of the group in tow. "We were so worried! But, I mean, we knew you'd be fine. Georgia loves stirring up trouble, but we knew you guys would never break the rules like that."

I feel a pang of guilt down in my stomach, and my eyes catch Cecily's for a moment. But I brush it away as quickly as I can. It's time for new beginnings.

Operation do-over.

"We're all really glad that you're not in trouble," Marcus says to Cecily.

My heart flips pancake-style inside my chest.

"Thanks, Marcus," Cecily says. "I really like your costume."

"I really wanted to go as Ron and Hermione, but Riley wanted to do Harry and Ginny."

"I would have picked Ron and Hermione, too," Cecily says, flashing a little smile my way. "They're the cooler couple . . . but, oh, well. Maybe next year."

Everyone keeps chatting away—everyone except Colin, who has yet to join us. I look back over at the sign-in table, and there he is. He and Georgia are arguing, and this time, there's no mistaking the outcome.

Georgia storms off in a huff, leaving Chloe alone and sad. She keeps staring over at the group, and I decide to take this opportunity free of Georgia to go say something to her.

"Chloe, you know you don't have to behave the way Georgia tells you to," I say.

"If I don't, she won't like me. And she's my friend."

"True friends don't force other friends to do things under the threat of not being friends anymore," I say. "True friends want you to be your own person, make your own decisions, and have your own opinions about things. And they support those."

"I don't know if I *have* opinions about things," Chloe says, and I immediately feel a rush of relief that I decided to come over here.

"Yes you do, Chloe. Georgia just doesn't let you share any of them."

And then I walk away. I want her to sit with that conversation for a bit, let it simmer. I'm not going to tell Chloe what to do like Georgia does. If she wants to see what life without her evil stepmother is like, she knows where to find us.

Just then, Ms. Tilly gets up on stage and takes the microphone. "Students of Limbo Central, welcome to the Ghostcoming Dance-a-Thon!"

Everyone cheers.

"We are thrilled that our Limbo Central football team won the game against North Limbo yesterday!" she continues. "Congratulations to the team! Now, without further ado, I will hand this over to our Ghostcoming chair, Georgia Sinclaire, to tell us about the dance-a-thon rules."

As Georgia climbs the stairs to the stage, someone appears behind me and whispers in my ear, "Hi!"

"Oh my god!" I say, jumping a little. I look back to see that it's Colin. "You seriously scared me."

"Well, I am a ghost—it's what we do."

"Ha-ha."

"So, listen," he says, "I'm really glad everything worked out with you and Cecily. I can't believe Georgia actually did that."

"Why exactly can't you believe it? I mean, she's done worse before and I'm sure she will again."

"Yeah, I guess. It's just, I've seen her when she's not being this way. She can be sweet, you know. I don't know why she does these things. I'm really sorry that she did what she did to you and Cecily. And I just told her it was officially over between us."

"Okay, well, that's good I guess, if that's what you want," I say, trying not to sound too excited. I mean, on the one hand, this is what I've been wanting since I got here. On the other, he's still kind of saying she's not as bad as I think she is. Dude?

Pick a side already.

"It is . . . what I want. And, I want something else, too," he says. "I want to be your partner for the dance-a-thon, if you'll have me?"

You've *got* to be kidding me.

THE LIMBO CENTRAL RULES

RULE #12:

Afterlife lasts forever. Forever is a very, very long time. This has its pros and its cons. On the one hand, it can give you many opportunities to make up for mistakes you have made and to right any wrongs. On the other, it can cause some ghosts to be selfish and take certain things for granted. Think carefully about where your priorities lie, and what type of ghost you want to become. Choose wisely.

Chapter Twelve
Dancing Queens

Colin is standing there, staring at me, waiting for my answer to his question—his totally amazing question that three days ago would have made me swoon so much that my knees would've buckled and I'd have probably started drooling.

But right now? I'm having a moment.

I like Colin and all, but why am I supposed to up and ditch Cecily just because he's decided to dump Georgia at the last second and needs a replacement partner for the dance-a-thon? I mean, I'm not saying Colin isn't nice—and I'm not saying I don't still like him. It's just . . . well, don't I deserve way more than this? If he wanted to go with me, he should have never said yes to Georgia and he should have accepted my invitation days ago.

Fine, he accepted Georgia supposedly so she would stop ganging up on me, which yes, is very nice. But also, that's just another way to give in to her. I mean, it's basically like blackmail. I'm a big girl—I can handle Georgia on my own. I don't need him fighting my battles for me. And besides all of that, he thinks I'm supposed to walk away from Cecily after everything that she's been through and leave her without a partner for the dance? That's, like, well . . .

Something Georgia would do.

"Uhm, Lucy?" Colin says, after what's probably been a whole five minutes of me staring up at the ceiling having an internal monologue.

"What?" I say, looking back at him.

"Look down," he says.

I look down and see that my dance-a-thon number tag, which used to be a nice crisp, white, has turned bright red and now has the words *So Georgia!* scrawled across it.

"Again?" I squeal.

Stupid ghost powers. Stupid emotions.

"I'm sorry," I tell Colin. "Under other circumstances, I would have loved to come to the dance with you. But I came here as Cecily's partner and I'm going to dance with her. Next time, if you want to go to a dance with me, ask me first. Or at least say yes when I ask you."

His face droops noticeably, like he just found out he didn't make the team. Kind of cute . . . but I'm staying strong!

After a few seconds of silent staring, he perks up a bit. "Deal. Okay, time to scrounge up a new partner—fast. I'll be back!" he says, and runs off.

"Okay, I missed all the rules talking to Colin," I whisper to Cecily. "Anything important I need to know?"

"Just don't stop dancing is pretty much the only main rule. You have to keep moving at all times."

"Got it."

"Oh, and Lou? Thanks for not ditching me."

"Me ditch you? Never."

The dance-a-thon finally begins, and everyone is out on the floor. I spy Georgia and her new partner, some beefy football player, who's now wearing the same outfit Colin was wearing but is clearly unhappy about it. I look for Chloe and Jonah—I assume they are near Georgia somewhere—but I don't see them. When I turn back toward Cecily and the rest of the group, Chloe and Jonah are right next to us.

"Thanks," Chloe says to me, "for what you said before."

"You're welcome."

"I'd like another chance to be your friend, if you'll give me one."

"Aren't second and third and fourth chances what Limbo is all about?" I say, smiling at her.

"Yeah, I guess you're right," she says. "After all, we do have forever to get it right."

"Let's hope it doesn't take *that* long."

Just as I take a bite into a second granola bar, Colin reappears in a brand-new get-up with Miles, one of Jessie and

Marcus's bandmates, by his side. Colin is Batman and Miles is the Joker.

"That was a quick change," I say.

"Batman always saves the day," Colin replies.

"And where are James and Trevor?" Cecily asks.

"They run the Limbo Central radio station so they're tonight's DJs. They're over there onstage, behind the spinning table."

"I had no idea they ran the station!" I say. "So they're the ones doing the morning announcements and stuff?"

"Yup," Colin says.

"Well, the music is awesome," Cecily chimes in.

That's when I get an idea.

"I'll be right back," I tell them.

Then I dance my way over to the front of the room and up the steps to the stage. I know the perfect way to win this dance-a-thon and take home those Ghostcoming crowns.

For the first forty-five minutes, everyone is on the dance floor and the energy is high. But after an hour or so, couples start losing steam and dropping out. Of course Georgia and her beefcake are still on the floor, but it's significantly less full now. By the beginning of hour three, there are ten couples left out of the fifty or so who entered. But I've already inhaled two sticks of string cheese and a bag of Cheetos, so I'm good to go.

Then I hear it. Our song.

Last year for our end of the City Steps summer camp recital, we got to choose a song to choreograph a dance to and we chose Taylor Swift's "Shake It Off." It was like a ballet/hip-hop hybrid dance, and it was the most fun we've ever had in our lives.

I look over at Cecily. "You ready to show these ghosts what we can really do?"

"For real?" she says.

"For real."

We start the routine and Chloe, Colin, and Mia help clear the floor for us. Within seconds, everyone else has stopped dancing and they are just watching us. But we don't even care, because we're having so much fun. We're twirling and doing splits and showing off our extensions and pointe work. There's this one part of the dance that Cecily does with a chair that I'm pretty sure blows everyone's mind. And then I finish it with a leap-pirouette combination across the floor, and the crowd erupts with applause.

Georgia storms off the floor.

Nailed it! (Again.)

"Ladies and gentlemen," Ms. Tilly says from the stage. "I believe we have our winning dance-a-thon couple! Ms. Chadwick and Ms. Vanderberg, please come up and claim your crowns."

Everyone is hooting and clapping as we ascend the stairs.

Since Georgia has up and vanished, Trevor has been given the honor of bestowing our crowns upon us. "Okay, so, who's the king and who's the queen?"

We all start laughing.

"Let's give it up for our Ghostcoming Dancing Queens!" James screams into the microphone, and we leave the stage and go back to join our friends.

The music starts up again and everyone comes back on the dance floor. I notice Marcus—sans his date—heading over toward Cecily. This gives me butterflies. While they talk, I go over to Mia and Trey.

"So, how does it feel to be, like, the cutest couple at the dance?" I ask them. "I mean, Trey, you're even holding her oxygen tank for her!! How did you get to be such a good boyfriend?"

"Lots and lots of mistakes," he jokes. "That's the cool thing about afterlife, man. You get a lot of—"

"Do-overs," I complete his sentence. "I've picked up on that."

"Your dance was wicked good," Mia says. "You and Cecily should start a dance club at Limbo for your required activity."

"You think we could?" I say. "I mean, I'd still like to do

photography, but a dance club would be awesome. And it would be WAY better than cheerleading, that's for sure."

"There are a bunch of rules about how to start a new club, but it's doable."

"Ha!" I laugh. "Of course there are. Would you join?"

"Please, with my two left feet? You're better off without me, I promise."

"Yeah, she can't dance," Trey chimes in. "The main reason I'm holding her oxygen tank is so she won't swing around and smack people with it."

"But I'll totally help you get it started."

"Thanks! I'm gonna go tell Cecily."

On my way over to her I bump into Colin.

"Congratulations!" he says, giving me a hug.

Just then Trevor switches the track to a slow song. I wonder if they planned it this way, but it's probably just a coincidence. Or maybe . . .

It's fate.

Either way? I'm happy to oblige.

Colin takes hold of my hand and we begin to dance together. I've never slow danced with a boy before, and I hope I'm doing it right. I know that sounds so ridiculous because, hello? I'm a dancer and all.

But this is different. Isn't it?

"I can't believe you two have only been here a little over a week," he says, as we sway back and forth. "I mean, you've already basically taken over the school."

"What?" I say. "That's crazy."

"You took on Georgia, you won Ghostcoming king and queen, and you're like the strongest, fastest-learning ghosts in the whole school."

"I don't know what to say," I reply, because I don't. "It's been a rough beginning, but I can't say I'm not feeling supremely proud of myself right now."

"Hey, can I ask you something, just between you and me?" he says.

I nod.

"Did Cecily really change her outfit all by herself before you got to the dance? I won't tell anyone either way, but you did seem pretty tired and you sure are eating a lot."

I want to tell him. After all, it was Colin's excellent tutoring that made this all possible. But I think of Cecily and decide to keep it to myself. At least, I decide not to *say* anything outright, that is.

I smile at him, raise my eyebrows, and tilt my head in that way that says, "I know but I'm not going to tell you."

"Wow," he says, "'the force is strong with you, young Skywalker.'"

"The *what* is *what* with me?" I ask.

"Dude, it's like the most famous line from *Star Wars*. You *have* to know this one. Darth Vader says it to Luke?"

"Is this before or after Boba Fett talks about the galaxy far, far away?"

"That's it, you're watching *Star Wars* with me," Colin says.

"It's a date," I say, but this time Georgia isn't anywhere in sight to object.

"Promise?" he asks.

"Cross my heart and hope to die."

Or whatever.

I leave Colin and continue my quest for Cecily, who I find over by the refreshments table.

"Marcus is getting me some punch."

"So, you two are getting along, huh?" I ask.

"Swimmingly!" she sings.

"That's awesome. I have more great news!" I say, excitedly. "Mia said that for our required activity thing we should start our own Dance Club! Wouldn't that be the best?"

"Oh my god, I had no idea we could just start our *own* club!"

"Well, Mia said there are a lot of rules."

"What else is new?"

"I know, but I'm sure we can handle it. And after our show tonight, I think we're going to have a lot of people who will want to join, don't you?"

"Definitely. So, what are the rules? Do we have to, like, write up something about why we think the club is important? Because there are like a million reasons why dance is important. Is there a deadline for when the forms are due? We only have like three weeks before we have to choose something, so we better get going on this, like, now!"

For a moment I thought she was just going to run out of breath and fall down dead.

Ha-ha.

"Cece! Take a break. We're not dealing with any of this tonight. Tonight, we are the queen and queen of Ghostcoming!" I say. "And we're going to fully enjoy it!"

"So . . . first thing tomorrow, then?" she asks.

"Marcus, take this dancing queen out on the floor, please," I say, jokingly.

There's nothing quite like dancing the night away with your friends. Don't get me wrong, it's great if there are cute boys at your side, too, but none of that is worth anything without a group of good girlfriends who've got your back.

Always.

Standing here watching Cecily, Mia, and Chloe smiling together, making jokes and letting loose, I can finally see *my* happily ever afterlife . . . and it looks, well, like the perfect do-over.

Keep reading for a sneak peek at

HAPPILY EVER AFTERLIFE

Crushed

"Okay, settle down," Coach Trellis says, and when I look up I notice Georgia is standing up in front of all of us next to Coach. "I've asked Georgia to help me teach the routine, since she has the most gymnastics experience from her cheerleading."

You've got to be kidding me.

Grrr.

I wish Coach had asked me to help. I mean, I did just win a dance-a-thon.

Whatever.

It's just a gym class. Besides, maybe this is a good thing? This way I can see what Georgia is like as a teacher, and what she'll be like as a captain. If she's as bad as I think she'll be, I can take that back to Cecily and use it to convince her to not join the Cheerleading squad.

"Okay, the first thing we're going to do is some floor poses," Georgia says. "Watch me and repeat what I do."

She gets down on her right knee and pulls her right foot toward the back of her hip, twisting her body all the way to the right.

Easy breezy.

Then she slowly lifts herself off the floor in the same exact position. For a few seconds, she just hovers there over the mat. Then she slowly drifts back down.

Ghost powers be darned.

"Okay," she says. "Let's see what you've got."

The class gets down on the floor and tries to mimic her, but most of them can't even get close.

"Ouch, this hurts!" cries one girl.

"Is it supposed to look all twisted like this?" asks another.

Georgia makes her way around the room, helping to pose the rest of the class.

After a few minutes, she comes up behind me. My pose is perfect, and I'm not just saying that. I do this stretch about twenty times a week before ballet class because it hits your quad muscles and your back at the same time.

Bring it, girl.

"Ladies," she calls out, "look at Lucy's positioning. She's doing this move perfectly. Try to copy her."

I'm in shock. There's no way Georgia's saying something nice just because. With this girl? There's always something. Unless . . . by some crazy chance, everything that happened at the dance made her rethink how she treats people?

Then she crouches down low behind me and whispers in my ear, "This thing between you and me? It isn't over. Not by a long shot."

Yeah.

And if Cecily joins the cheerleading squad, I can tell you exactly what Georgia is going to do:

1. Shower Cecily with fake attention
2. Weasel her way into becoming Cecily's BFF
3. Enact some other kind of revenge that I can't think of right now but I know will be THE WORST

Georgia's words keep echoing in my head, and the more I think about her, the more frustrated I get. What should be a gentle hover a few inches above the ground turns into me shooting myself up in the air like a cannonball and hitting my head on the ceiling.

Ouch.

"Lucy, please be careful," Georgia reprimands, as if I did it on purpose. "As you can see, integrating your ghost skills with your former life skills isn't quite as easy as some might think."

I can't believe I'm actually about to say this, but . . . Georgia is (GASP!) right.

By the time class ends, I'm so amped up about our dance club idea—not to mention bruised—that I can barely think straight.

"Oh ladies!" Georgia calls out as class ends. "I have one small announcement, please, before you go. I just wanted to remind you that tryouts for the Limbo Central Cheerleading Squad are taking place outside on the football field on Wednesday evening at five o'clock! It's going to be a great year, and we're looking to fill a few spots on the squad. I noticed a lot of promise out there today—so please come and try out!"

I don't know what hits me, but suddenly I open my mouth and say: "And, if you're looking to be a part of something even cooler than cheerleading—to be part of a creative group that listens to one another and works together as a team—come join our brand-new Limbo Central Dance Club! Oh, and you don't need to try out for our club, because we're inclusive, not exclusive. If you sign up, you're in!"

If we were playing volleyball now? That serve would have gone straight to *her* head!

Guess I need to figure out this whole starting-your-own-supernatural-club thing.

Like, now.

Orli Zuravicky is a writer, an editor, and an amateur interior designer, which basically means she likes to paint stuff in her apartment. She has been in children's publishing for fifteen years and has written over sixty-five books for children. She hopes to write sixty-five more. She lives her happily ever after (life) in Brooklyn, New York.